THE FUTURE OF NOTHING

JH Tomen

ISBN: 979-8-9862909-5-9

ISBN-13:

Dear Reader,

Welcome to The Future of Nothing, a sci-fi collection set in the 2040s, in a world forever changed by climate disaster. Still, my goal is to look at humanity from a place of hope – imagining a world where we finally live in harmony with nature, becoming who we're truly meant to be.

You can find this collection in web form too, giving you a place more fully experience this world. After each story, you'll find additional resources where you can learn more about key technologies and explore ways to get involved in shaping the world we deserve. If these stories grab you, feel free to read more at https://jhtomen.com/the-future-of-nothing/ Enjoy!

JH Tomen

To what we still have. To who we can still be.
et tui amóris in eis ignem accénde
renovábis fáciem terræ

Art by Alyssa Dennis (@alyssadennisstudios)
Cover by Karl Nilsson (@sigvardnilsson)
Editing by A.K. Edits (@AdotKEdits)
Copyright © 2024 JH Tomen

The Bridge

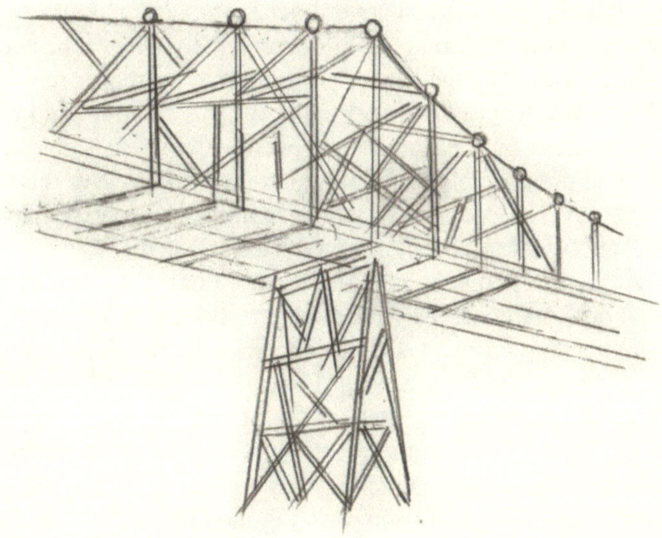

I steered my little boat around the scrum of other ships, only one hand on the wheel as I hurried through a hasty breakfast. I hadn't exactly had time to stop, but it wasn't often my work took me through the Mackinac Straits, and I wouldn't have been able to forgive myself if I hadn't grabbed a pastie. Now that so many people lived up here, you could get flavors I could have only dreamed of growing up.

That morning, I'd grabbed a particularly good black daal. I'm sure my great-grandfather would have thought them a sacrilege against the pasties of his youth — he refused to budge from beef or chicken — but then again, immigration begets innovation. Pasties wouldn't even be here without Cornish immigrants in the 1840s, and I wasn't about to forsake my taste buds for some misplaced sense of propriety. Besides, I'm pretty sure my Poppy wouldn't have thought his great-granddaughter could be a boat captain, either...

A coast guard trawler passed me on the starboard side, letting out a friendly double honk. Tossing back the last of my pastie, I honked back, turning the wheel as I headed for the bridge. I was getting plenty of friendly honks now with the Census emblem painted on my hull. Not everyone had been friendly when I started asking questions, but people in the straits sure were, especially now that I'd started running supplies as I made my rounds. With accurate carbon pricing, it wasn't like you could do overnight shipping anymore.

Today, though, I had official government cargo, laden down with vials of the new antibiotics coming out of Traverse City. They'd be excited to see me at the hospital on the island, the biggest in the region now, though hopefully the residents would feel the same. I'd been making my way up the northwest coast for months, and even with my incredibly winning smile, I'd had more than a few doors slammed on me. Not that I could blame them... The losses we'd all been through were so incredibly personal. Who was I to turn their loved ones into statistics?

And yet, there was power in statistics, too. For me, there was *hope* in finding out how many people were alive, even if it also involved finding out how many people were dead. Besides, with the rebuilding underway, it was about time we did a census. Even if it was 2042, we certainly hadn't been able to do one in 2030, and a lot had happened over the past twelve years. Just looking at the coastline, you'd be a fool not to notice.

There were thousands of new buildings dotting the hills of Mackinaw City. Even as the water had risen, pushing the coast back, they were all full of families who'd heard about the growth in the region. We had plenty of refuge towers, of course, but now people were just coming to work, excited about the new orchards they were putting in as the climate stabilized. Even though we were only a quarter of the way through the census, there had to be at least a million people here between Emmet and Cheboygan County. Just a casual twentyfold increase from before the crisis... Even if the estimates were right that the country's population had been cut by two-thirds, it was astounding. Now we just had to figure out who all was there.

I passed by the northern district's carbon towers, the blue lights still blinking in the early morning sun. I began to turn my wheel again, the towers my final reminder to start following the channel markers more closely. Traffic had quadrupled in recent years, and if I didn't stay between the buoys as I approached the island, my little rig would no doubt be swallowed by the dozens of freighters passing through.

I went under the bridge, my boat entering its shadow. The whoosh of trucks sounded overhead, pushing over the metal grates as their drivers headed to the UP. The trucks felt almost too close now with the rise in the water level, but it felt good to pass beneath them all the same. Even after everything we'd been through, the bridge still stood after ninety years, a vital artery in the new heart of civilization. Though it was funny to think my home could be so vital to the recovery. It must have been what it had felt like in the copper boom of the 1800s, when they'd almost put the capitol up here, the last time our population had rivaled Detroit's.

I followed the blue buoys, their blinking lights guiding me north toward the island. The waters were calm for the moment — the winter storms finally subsided — though the winds were strong, the massive wind farm off of Bois Blanc a blur of white as the turbines spun. Though I couldn't complain. The wind was what made the hospital such a hub. Even if an island would have been inconvenient twenty years ago, the regained supremacy of boats ensured it was one of the easiest places to reach in the region.

I finally reached the docks, the concrete stretching out from the fort. I used to come here as a girl, and it still baffled me to look down through the crystal-clear waters at the remains of the old downtown. I remembered walking there with my gran, intent on avoiding the shops full of fudgies as she dragged me to the oldest one on the island. Actually, I'd just heard the week before that someone was making fudge again — the chocolate imports finally stable enough — and I made a note to hunt it down. After a hundred and forty years of making fudge — with a forced break in between — it'd be rude *not* to eat it.

The dock sergeant noticed me coming in, flashing a light on the military section on the west end. I pulled into a slip in the middle, a dockhand jumping on board to tie me off. I switched off the engine, putting my coat back on as I opened the cabin door.

"You're the one with the antibiotics, right?" the sergeant asked, shaking my hand as I climbed onto the dock.

"Sure am," I said. "Though I'll need a two-day pass, lots of questions for the Census Bureau."

"No problem," he said, scratching out a pass for me.

He tore it from a pad, the little blue piece of paper scribbled with the dates I'd be allowed to stay on the island. Two days felt incredibly short after all that sailing, but I wasn't about to complain. Plenty of boats would be coming behind me, and I wasn't about to hog the island.

It took another hour of wrangling with the dockhands — and a kerfuffle with the hospital workers who'd run down from the hospital behind the fort — but finally, I was free to wander on my own. I headed for land, the horse-drawn wagon they'd sent for the antibiotics clearing a path for me.

Behind the old white stone of the fort, the new city stretched into the sky. Miraculously, it housed nearly ten thousand people, the island's population of humans finally above that of its horses, though they'd at least managed to keep cars banned. I mean, what would you do with a car anyway? The island had lost two miles of its mere eight-mile diameter from before, and with the old forests thankfully still protected, there'd hardly be anywhere to drive a car, let alone park it.

I started up the new main street, the shops all full of people as the road wound its way up the limestone cliffs. At some point, I'd just start asking questions. Our records weren't good enough for me to seek out specific houses, but at this point, I was just trying to confirm the population we'd guessed from the voucher system anyway.

But I wasn't really in any kind of rush either. I'd sleep on the boat like always, so I didn't have to try and find a place to stay, and the sun felt good against the dark blue of my uniform. But more than anything, it just felt good to be around so many people again. My questions were always a bit morbid — how many had been lost from each household, how they'd died, and so many other terrible things — but for the moment, I could bask in the present, surrounded by the living.

"Hey there," a voice called to me.

I turned, finding a man in a white apron looking down at me from an open window. The sign above the door said it was a bakery.

"You from the census?" he asked. He looked older, around my father's age if he'd still been alive.

"I am," I said carefully, always ready with my best explanations — or excuses, depending on who you asked… But the man ended up smiling, pointing toward the door.

"Come on this way," he said, "I wanna be the first one you talk to. I'll give you some bread for your trouble too."

"It's no trouble," I said, laughing. "Believe it or not, they pay me to do this, though I won't say no to fresh bread."

I went around the porch, a big smile on my face. Maybe the island would be easier than my other stops. After all, how could you feel bad with the breeze at your back and the clopping of horses in your ears? I had plenty of questions to ask, of course, but for once, it felt like I had answers too. Life felt *good* again, and more importantly, it felt like it was here to stay, whether or not I counted it.

Tide Work

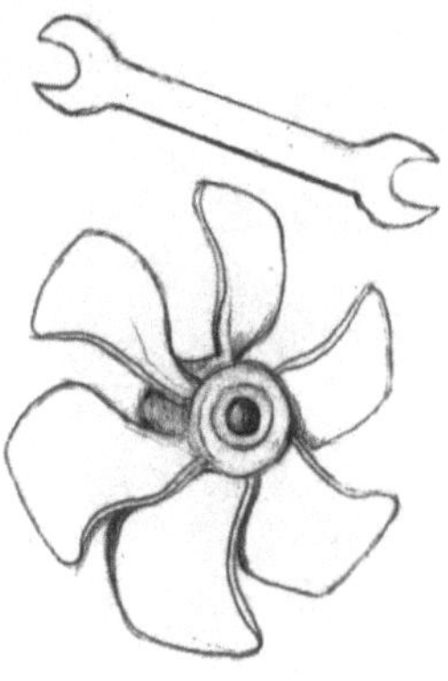

The aluminum ladder felt warm under my fingers, the metal already taking to the summer sun despite an afternoon spent under the water. Still, I tried to keep my focus on the rungs beneath me. As much as I wanted to look at the lines of prehistoric rock on the wall, the ladder had been designed in a hurry, and it wasn't graded for daydreaming.

Behind me, though, I knew the Bay of Fundy was pulling out, billions of gallons of water being leeched from the basin by the moon.

"Those tides are like eight thousand trains!" my supervisor had shouted at orientation. "Or twenty-five million horses. One wrong move, and you'll be trampled!"

I couldn't really imagine that many horses, let alone what kind of power they had, but I was excited to be there all the same. I'd signed up on a whim, calling the number on a flyer in the lobby of my refugee center.

I wasn't the first to leave, of course. With all the 'great rebuilding' fervor everywhere, plenty of my friends had left for other opportunities. It's not that I didn't want a change of scenery — or more pay than the pittance I usually got for my maintenance work — but something else had drawn me here. Maybe it was the trees, some of the largest forests remaining after the fires, the pines dotting the stone like fur on the world's back. Or maybe it was just the bay itself, a picture on the flyer showing this alien cavern, a place to walk where there was water only hours before. Either way, it was completely different from anything I'd ever known, and it was a way to forget what I'd lost, the sand and saguaros from home I'd never see again.

I knew I wasn't like the other men on the crew. They all had that haunted look I'd grown so used to seeing at the refugee center. But I hadn't lost anyone — except the Earth, which, of course, I felt keenly. Still, my life had been so hollow in the before, empty and silent. I'd had close friends growing up, sure, but they'd all moved away for one thing or another — college, girlfriends, jobs. So, it felt like my life had only really begun in the after, surviving by instinct and assistance while I waited for something new.

And this *was* new. They were calling it one of the first 'energy positive' projects of the rebuilding, set to provide 2 GW a day when it was done, basically returning to the capacity of fossil production in the area in the before. We were finally stepping beyond our own destruction into something new, circular even, like the tides themselves, finally at peace with the rhythms of our world — or so we hoped, anyway.

And I loved every second of it. As the whistle blew to signal the start of the shift, I crouched down, beginning my slow march across the bed of the bay, inspecting another hundred yards of cable. The foremen liked to call my crew the 'sea urchins,' laughing at the spikes of tools on our backs as we edged along the lines, but the work suited me just fine. I always tried to go slowly, letting my mind empty as I divided the minutes of my shift as evenly as I could — what I estimated to be a required pace of a yard every two minutes.

I started with the first section, making sure the joints were tight and the casing had no rips before feeling each segment of the cable. Up ahead, I could see one of the skilled crews — engineers, technicians, welders — working on a tidal turbine. It was like a spaceship, the turbines lifting like thrusters from the metal body where it was attached to the sea floor.

Unlike me, they worked urgently, forced to finish an entire turbine during each shift before the tides came rolling back in.

Their job certainly had more drama — and glory, presumably — but I liked to think my work was just as vital. Sea urchin or not, *most* jobs weren't glamorous, but if no one did them, things fell apart. In the before, people seemed to think there was something shameful about that, as if the pyramid was meant to be inverted. But now, after things had fallen apart, I think we could see that more clearly. Because for a time, everything had stopped, and anyone still willing to do a vital job had probably saved a life by doing it. Maybe 'normal' was a thing of the past, but everyone doing their jobs together was probably the closest we'd ever get.

I let my mind go blank, letting the tide of routine sweep into my mind. It was so freeing to have a task I could do without question. I'd been fairly young when things started to fall apart, in the first year at my office job, but all I remember is a sort of dread. Every project felt like a performance review, a chance to either "brand yourself" or be destroyed by another cycle of Machiavellian corporate restructuring. And in the end, after all the scheming we'd all done, none of us had made it. One day, they'd told us all to go, handing us orange boxes with smiling cats on them, stuffed to the gills with branded cups and hats.

"We'll see you soon!" they'd said cheerfully, locking the doors behind us. I never went back, though. No one did.

Here, in the Bay of Fundy, though, I finally felt some measure of satisfaction with my work. We did two shifts a day, one around seven in the morning and the other around seven at night, taking advantage of both low tides. We finished around ten when the water came back, and the company fed us in a giant tent. It was…fantastic. I wasn't so naive as to think life would always be this easy, but for now, in the rebuilding, everything was a scramble. Even the supervisors did something on every crew, and there were no performance reviews. One day, the work would be done, so there was no need to fire us ahead of time for quarterly profits. You either laid the cable or you didn't. That was it.

Near the end of my shift, with ten yards to go and the sun low in the sky, I finally found a snag in the line. I felt it before I saw it, a dent in the plating of the cable. The cables were coated with six or seven layers: polyethylene, Kevlar, banded stainless steel, all of it designed to avoid being pulled apart by the currents. But sometimes, a perfectly shaped rock might get dragged across the sea floor, where it would fly through the cable trench and dent the line. It would take a lot to sever the line, of course, and one day, when the budget ran out, perhaps they would simply run the turbines until they gave out. But for now, they wanted — *needed* — this thing to work.

"Line!" I called out, waving a red flag over my head. A spotter up ahead waved his back at me, whistling for an engineer to head my way. One of the engineers I knew well eventually made his way to me, lugging a huge bag of tools on his shoulder. I pointed out the spot to him before getting back to my inspections, not wanting to outstay my usefulness — which, despite my satisfaction with the work, was limited.

It still amazed me we could run electricity from the sea floor into Halifax. Even with all the advancements we'd made over the last two hundred years, it was too much for my non-engineering mind to fathom, I guess. Someone had told me that the first transatlantic cable had only been able to transmit forty words a minute. But that at least had a kind of intuitive analog to it. You hit the button on the telegraph and the electricity runs sort of slowly — by modern standards, anyway — to the other side. It wasn't the lightning-fast stuff we were building here, with electrons running its length in an eye blink. And yet, here I was, just another peg in the process of humanity.

"Good spotting," the engineer finally said, nodding at me. "That was deeper than it looked."

I turned, looking at where he'd put in a patch, making the outside of the cable smooth again before it could buckle or breach.

"I don't know if I'm good luck or bad," I said. "That's my fifth this week."

"Well, in my line of work, bad things always happen. The luck is catching 'em. Besides, it's a hell of a lot of water we're dealing with."

"True enough," I said, nodding as he left.

Soon, I finished the line, and the whistle blew to signal the tide had returned to the point where we had to ship out. Luckily, the skilled crew had finished nearby, the engineers hastily wrapping up their test spins on the turbine rotors. Soon, we'd be back at dinner, the energy from that rotor filling the peninsula with light.

I turned to go, pulling my tools over my shoulder. The other crews would take a bit longer — the water sometimes nipping at their heels — but I didn't mind climbing out alone. Sea urchin or not, it still felt like I was part of something. Like the forest above, you needed creatures who climbed up trees and others who ate dead logs. But for once, I knew what I was, what purpose I served, and I was proud of it.

A Sort of Parent

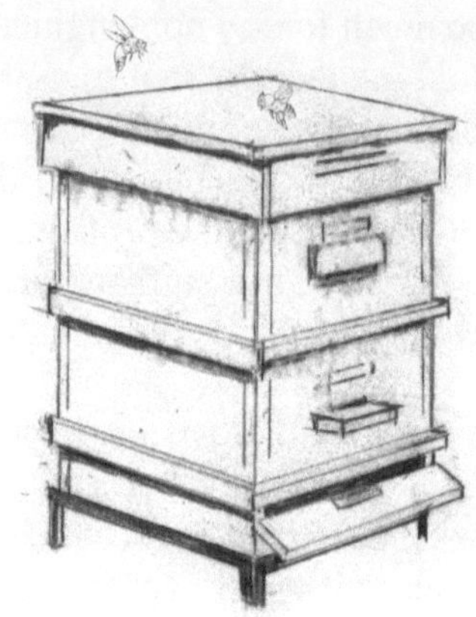

Alloparenting.

The word finally came to me. It had been years since I'd thought of it — of anything that technical, I suppose. I think before everything fell apart, it had given me hope, a sort of path forward for humanity. We had to live with less: fewer children, fewer houses, fewer things. Someone probably had to have kids — replacement rate and all that, not to mention all those deaths — but what about the rest of us? Living the same isolated, individual-obsessed lives we'd had before clearly wasn't going to work. But if we *connected,* being a part of one big life all together, perhaps we could solve for some of the cracks in the way we lived.

Now, it's just what we call parenting, I guess. If you were lucky enough to still have loved ones left alive — and I mean the ones you chose — it had just become the way things were. You lived together, ate together, somebody taught the kids how to read. But I found myself searching for a term again, searching for something to validate what I had become. Most of the kids in the house called me Uncle, but what was an uncle anyway? Somedays, I felt like I'd entered a non-place, where I didn't recognize myself and no one else did either.

"Why'd you pick me up anyway? Where's my mom?"

"Your mom…" I started to answer before I stopped myself. I shot a look back at Lill. That was a hell of a tone to take with an adult. Still, she was unfazed, cocking an eyebrow at me before she went back to whacking the bushes with a stick. We were on the path back to the house, taking the shortcut through the woods. Fourteen or not, she was the smartest of the kids, and she knew she had my number. *'What the hell are you gonna do about it?'* that look seemed to say.

"She got called to the dam," I continued, relenting. "Something about a broken rotor."

Lill muttered something under her breath.

"Don't turn this around on me," I continued, forcing myself to find the stomach to confront a surly teen. "You're the one who got in a fight. Why'd you hit that girl?"

She mumbled something to herself, which sounded like it included some choice swear words, though I decided to let that slide, basically a sailor myself. I stopped, turning to face her on the path as I folded my arms — as if that would somehow protect me from her sharp tongue.

"Come on, Lill, I can't help you if I don't know. And you know I got these old man ears. Just tell me what happened."

She *almost* smiled. She loved making fun of my ears — affectionately, of course. I'd worked on the rescue boats too long, and I could barely hear anything after being next to the engine all those years. Still, almost smiling was hardly the real thing, and her jaw bulged, clearly grinding her teeth.

"Fine," she said, rolling her eyes as she walked ahead of me on the path. Still, when she spoke, she at least did so loud enough for me to hear.

"They all think I'm weird. They all live in the row houses — the little pampered airheads — and I'm stuck on the farm with who knows how many parents. They always look down on me, but today, they started following me down the hallway, making a buzzing sound. *Buzz, buzz, buzz.* So I snapped. Still, I'm not sorry. They can kick me out for all I care. I should be working anyway; mom always says so."

Her mom most certainly did not always say so, but I held my tongue. There was no way to insert yourself into the thousands of wounds generated between a mother and daughter. All you could do was try to love them both. Besides, it must be hard. I'd been bullied too — a thousand years ago — and while there were plenty of other families like ours dotting the hills, she was the only one at her school. We were the closest to town, which meant the other families all had jobs at the depot, with single family housing to match.

"I'm sorry," I finally said when she finished. "We'll figure something out together."

She shot me a look over her shoulder. *Together* might sound like a threat, but I meant it in a good way. I'd go to bat for her, find a way to deal with those horrible kids without embarrassing her further. I just had to hope she'd get all that context as I used as few words as possible to keep from scaring her off.

We reached the end of the woods, the sound of the Illinois River passing through the trees. On the left, our giant field opened up, the hundreds of hives like buzzing statues as the bees wandered the fields in search of pollen. Beyond that, on the hill, our house poked its head over the trees, a handful of the lights on as the other aunts and uncles busied about the house.

"I have to stop to check on one of the hives," I said, turning back to Lill. "You can stay with me or go up to the house, but I can't promise you won't get a talking to up there."

She looked up at the house, weighing her odds.

"I'll stay with you," she said with a sigh.

"Thought so."

She could give me a bad rap if she wanted to, but she knew I was the easy one. Even if it meant I had no spine, it still gave me a sort of satisfaction. If she turned out alright as an adult — which didn't seem like a stretch, knocking that girl's teeth out notwithstanding — it might give me a shot at being her favorite uncle. And if she didn't turn out... Well, the others had certainly done their best.

We turned into the hives, the giant triangles giving off shade from the afternoon sun. Even after all this time, I still liked to look at them, the federal models like some kind of spaceship in my own back yard. They looked even more surreal when it flooded, the hives rising on their poles as they floated out of harm's way.

"Why do we have to do this?" Lill asked, still swatting her stick through the air — which made me pray she didn't accidentally hit a bee. They were all used to our scent, of course, but they wouldn't — and shouldn't — take kindly to being smacked by a teen.

"This was the deal when the government gave us the deed to this place. We do something with the floodplain, they give us a house. It sure as hell beats a mortgage."

"What's a mortgage?" she asked, the curiosity actually entering her voice again, the tone I'd grown to miss as she left childhood behind. It wasn't totally impossible to resurrect — she'd been obsessed with the past when she was younger — but it still struck me as a breath of fresh air after so many months of teenage angst. Not that I was any better at her age…

"It's the way we used to get houses. You'd borrow the money from a bank and take like thirty years to pay it back. I guess it wasn't a bad deal, but it was kind of like a prison sentence too. Kept me in an office job I hated, kept your mom working at the oil company."

"When she wanted to be a water engineer?"

"I don't know," I said, continuing down the row of hives. "I don't know that it was water necessarily, but I think she wanted to be any other kind of engineer, one that wasn't hurting people."

Lill was quiet after that. Sometimes she liked to use her mom's work in the oil fields as a kind of weapon, a wedge to give her the moral superiority teens so crave. Even if she didn't totally know what oil was — thank heavens for that — she knew it made her mother feel impossibly guilty. But now… She seemed to take the information whole, part of the fabric of her parents' identities.

We finally reached the end of the row, the bucket I'd been filling with honey still waiting where I'd left it when I ran off to the school. Lill flopped down in the shade, and I let her. Sometimes, it helped to do an activity together, but not today. I popped the lid on the hive, working quietly while she stared at the sky. After a while, though, she groaned, burying her head in her knees.

"I hate this place," she said, her voice muffled. "I just wanna run away."

I stopped, wiping my brow as I forced myself to suck in a deep breath. I stayed by the hive but turned, squatting down to her level.

"I get that," I said.

"No, you don't," she said quietly. "You love it here."

"Sure," I said, "but this is something I chose, and you didn't get to. Besides, I was the same when I was a teen. You're supposed to hate the box we put you in. That's how society changes, it's just…"

I paused, looking around at the hives. They looked so impossibly beautiful to me, like nothing else I'd ever seen. Suddenly, I felt one of those rare waves of honesty surging up. One she could use against me later, but one she deserved all the same.

"Before, I hated my life, too. I spent all my time wishing I was free, wishing things were different. But I never did anything about it. I think

I was afraid of living. We all were back then, at least a little. We had to do everything so…perfectly, just to make sure we didn't starve to death when we were old. But we starved anyway, and now…I wish I'd done things differently."

Lill lifted her head, meeting my eyes for just a second before she looked away, staring back at the sky.

"What do you wish you'd done differently?" she asked quietly.

"Well," I said, sighing as an old face came back into my mind, "there was a woman, an artist. We dated for a while, and I loved her, I think, but I never gave us a chance. She was too free, too chaotic, and I didn't think it would work out. But knowing what I know now, knowing that *nothing* worked out… I guess I just wish I'd spent more time with her. Or maybe I just wish she and I could have jumped to right here, to this field, to these bees. I have everything I ever wanted now except for her."

Lill looked up at me, considering me anew as I smiled awkwardly, the embarrassment catching up with me. What was my point? Did I even have one? Was I breaking the adult fourth wall or just spouting off more useless advice?

"What was her name?" she asked.

"Lisa," I said, just above a whisper, like the name was a spell I didn't dare utter. Still, this was about Lill, not me, and I pushed ahead, desperate to use her brief window of attention to help her somehow.

"Look, when you finish school, you can do whatever you want. You can leave, even. I'd support you, help you explain to your mom and whatever else. Just…don't put yourself in a box. Don't do what I did, convincing yourself there's only one way you can be. Even if you run away — even if that's the total opposite of me living a safe, meaningless life before — it would still be a box. One day, your mom will get off your case, and those kids who give you trouble at school will learn to at least pretend they aren't little shits. You can go, but if you want to, you can stay. Just be who you really are, and the rest will sort itself out."

She took a deep breath, looking toward the river, but when she looked back, she actually smiled.

"I guess that's actually kind of good advice."

"It is?"

"Maybe, but don't tell anybody."

She stood, taking my honey bucket and slinging it over her shoulder as she headed toward the house. I chuckled, putting the cover back on the hive, the bees buzzing happily around my head. Maybe I really was a parent. An *alloparent.* Still, I was *something,* and that felt a whole lot better than anything I'd ever been before.

Towers

I looked down into the water tower, just catching the shine of the water in the darkness. It was still about half-filled, but it was going to be another hot week, and the people who lived below would surely appreciate the extra water for their gardens. I leaned over the edge of the roof where my team was waiting below.

"Alright!" I called down. "Fire her up!"

They started working the pump, pushing water from the wagon up to the third floor. After triple-checking the hose connection, I turned, looking across the roofs where another dozen water towers sat waiting in a near-perfect row. This was my favorite street, one of the only places in the city where the houses were close enough in size for all the towers to line up like this. Still, no two were alike, most of the owners having painted their own little murals on the aluminum siding.

My daughter and I had painted the one on our house, too, even if our street was less…participatory. She was only five, but she'd still drawn me with a hose in my hand.

"Mommy does the water," she'd said.

It made my heart swell with pride just thinking about it, though maybe it was to be expected with how obvious I was about my love for this job — hell, I'd even gotten a tattoo of a water tower on my arm, the old kind from the 1800s with the metal ridges. But it felt fitting. Even with the new aluminum models, I felt like a time traveler, bringing back everything we'd lost one gallon of water at a time. And if that let me live in the present, if it let me have a *daughter* — and the confidence I'd actually live to see her grow up — I'd wear my silly tattoo proudly.

It wasn't like I didn't have nightmares — everyone still seemed to — but they didn't linger like they used to. In fact, when I wake up now, I can hardly remember my dreams at all. Maybe it's some sort of trauma response. Like my own mother and the way she used to talk about COVID. She called it a time warp, a narrow funnel that wiped your memories away. I was too small to remember, but she'd always said it had changed me too: the games I played with my toys, the things I talked about.

I guess the mind can only take so much suffering. But forgetting can be healthy, too. What good would it do for me to talk about 'trophic collapse' and 'degenerative heat cycles?' All I really need is a vague impression of those times and the lesson I learned: we got through them together. All my work on the neighborhood emergency council, the tallies, dividing the supplies. As traumatic as those times had been, they hadn't been some machismo fantasy either, everyone shooting at each other as they fought over the last chocolate bar. We'd survived by clinging to each other in the storm, and I wasn't about to let go just because the sun had started shining.

"Rice up!" someone on my crew called.

"Heard," I called back, coming to the edge where we'd attached the winch, five big bags of rice rising in their metal basket.

Before the rice reached the top, I took one last peek into the water tower, making sure it wasn't about to overflow.

"Ten more good pumps," I called down, coming back to the side as the rice reached the top.

Squatting, I pulled up each bag of rice, carrying it to the metal bin next to the water. They were surprisingly similar in weight to my daughter, actually, though whether lifting her was good practice or just more punishment on my muscles remained to be seen. Still, I wouldn't trade it for anything. Soon, she'd be too big for me to lift, and then she'd even get to be a teenager in a way I never did. Even as it would surely break my heart, I wanted her to have that, refusing hugs and stomping off to her room like I'd only seen in the movies.

Finally, the sound of the water started to change in pitch, the air in the tower running out as it filled. Still, I had no fear of it overflowing now. I trusted my crew, and when I said ten pumps, it would be exactly ten. I looked through the hatch one last time, the rippling water beginning to still. It was so close now, I could see the shimmer of my face in its surface. It was too dark to make out details, but I didn't need a mirror to know that I was smiling.

Permanent Winter

"Permanent winter?" she asked from the seat next to me, clearly horrified. It honestly took me by surprise. I'd forgotten what it was like growing up in the Midwest, where everyone acted like they were allergic to winter. Personally, I'd always longed for it — with the exception of three o'clock sunsets, I suppose — my body far more suited to the cold. Being hot was a curse, an inescapable pain, and one we'd spent the last two centuries trying to make permanent. But I guess with the warming of winter over the years, people had stopped complaining. Or perhaps they just felt lucky to be alive… Either way, this was a reminder: we were going back to better times, when weather was something you could complain about casually again.

"Yeah," I said, chuckling, "it's not for everybody. But I love it."

"One winter's enough for me," she said, shaking her head as she went back to her book. "And Perth doesn't even get that cold. But good on you; somebody's gotta do it."

We were in a solar eVTOL, the plane's blades whirring through the windows. I'd come over to Australia on an airship, but the company was running these planes for the last leg of the trip, the eVTOL more efficient for the shorter range. Below us, the outback stretched into forever, the baked soil red and desolate. We'd be in Perth soon, but I wanted one more look out the window, anything to clear my head before another full day of work.

Not that I disliked my job. If anything, I was grateful. Most importantly, it gave me a chance to switch hemispheres every six months — accessing the 'permanent winter' my plane companion had been so skeptical of. But this was going to be one of my biggest jobs yet, and it would likely take the entire season, perhaps until summer threatened me once more. I was in Perth to fix a single substation, but I'd stay in the country afterwards, installing another twenty.

Through the window, I could see the blades turning upward as the pilots prepared for the approach. By the time we reached the landing zone, they were completely upright, allowing the plane to make its vertical landing. There was a light rain as we touched down on a perfect circle in the grass, the eVTOL pads like crop circles as they dotted the outside of the airport. I could see the terminal in the distance, though it was hard to make out through the airship strips where the grass was allowed to grow wild.

"Remember when airports were all concrete?" I asked the woman as we waited to deplane. She was younger than me, but by the way she frowned, looking out the window, she must have been too young to remember.

"I don't think so," she said, smiling apologetically. She'd spoken to me first, asking me to help her get her bag into the bin, but I still hoped I wasn't becoming the kind of old man who forced his stories on everyone. "By the time I was in middle school, the airports were shuttered, and by the time I was flying, they had airships and biozones."

"Makes sense," I said, stepping into the aisle where I pulled her bag back down. "You didn't miss much; these are better."

I found my driver near baggage claim, a low-slung hat on his head and a sign with my company's logo.

"Noah," he said, shaking my hand.

He led me back to his truck, making an attempt to ask me how the flight was even as he sped ahead, my ears just barely catching each word he tossed over his shoulder.

"This is her," he said, throwing my luggage unceremoniously in the back. Not that I kept anything important in there... To my surprise, smooth jazz started blasting the moment the car was on. My dad had listened to smooth jazz back in the day. I couldn't relate at the time, never understanding why he didn't listen to songs with lyrics. Though, I suppose I was younger then, before work gave me my own stress complex, skyrocketing my interest in wordless melodies.

From the airport, we turned away from the city, heading toward the hills and Mundaring. The city was already doing well enough on their adaptation projects, and I was being brought in to help reclaim the suburbs.

"I reckon you're the only bloke this side of the planet who can fix a heat pump substation this size, eh?"

"Hardly," I said. "Just the only one at my company willing to travel."

"Now that's a concept. Must be nice."

I smiled, going back to looking out the window. I was getting older, but it's not like there were pensions anymore. So, until we fixed things, I'd stay on the road, avoiding the heat as best I could.

As we left the airport, heading east on Koongamia, the fields outside the window were suddenly completely white. Like the sails to some kind of massive ship, shade cloths covered the landscape, climbing the hills as they reflected the sun back into space.

"Quite a sight, eh?" Noah asked, following my gaze.

"It is," I mumbled, still mesmerized. I shook my head, turning away. "I'd heard, but... I guess everyone's mitigation is different."

"Suppose so," Noah said. "Sure saved lives on the bad days."

We rode the rest of the way in silence, until we were well into the hills. Suddenly, the traffic on the Great Eastern Highway slowed, pulling into a sort of roadside checkpoint, where armed guards were inspecting the cars. Noah flashed a badge, and we were waved right through, turning off the highway and into town.

"Is it restricted up here?" I asked, looking back at the checkpoint through the truck's rear window.

"Well, we're trying to keep the right people in here. Won't be long before we're off credits, after all."

"Oh," I said, slumping back into my seat.

It's not like I'd never seen corruption before. In the darkest times, there was hoarding and bribery. But there were coups and assassinations too, and it felt like we'd finally reached a sort of equilibrium, everyone pulling in the same direction. After five decades of misinformation and science denial, there was finally evidence in front of your face that we needed to work together. And for the most part — minus a few millenarian movements — people had.

But I guess good things don't last forever. Like the post-war period a century ago, we were switching from guns to butter, and not everybody was going to get a slice. Still, it made me horribly sad. The only silver lining to the collapse — for me, anyway — was that I'd thought we would once and for all free ourselves of the golden handcuffs. It was a shame people were so easy to put them back on. But I guess even if you walled off a town, you couldn't deny the truth: we need each other. Even these new suburbs were going to rely on advanced cooling — at least until we all got back below two degrees — and you simply couldn't do that without a society willing to back you up.

At the first big clump of buildings, we pulled off the road, following a dirt track through the bush until we came to a massive concrete structure dug into the hillside. Built into the shape of a giant hourglass, I could hear the whir of the blades even before the truck stopped. This was the second largest heat pump substation my company had, and I'd honestly always wanted to see it. The sheer audacity of pumping cold air into some five thousand homes seemed like just the kind of thing we ought to be doing after everything we'd been through.

"Tools inside?" I asked, opening the door as soon as we stopped.

"Sure are," Noah said. "Guess you'll let me know what you need?"

"I will," I said, closing the door behind me.

For the next few hours, it would be just me and the machine. I stepped through a porthole in the concrete tube and onto a metal platform. The lead fan was still spinning, but the report said capacity had dropped 10% and no one knew why. Unfortunately — or fortunately for an aestophobic repairman — the substation had hundreds of parts. It was like the heat pump behind your house, only, well…the *size* of your house. And that meant the compressors, evaporators, and condensers all had a dozen units put together and operating in tandem. A single fuse could have blown, taking out a tenth of the units. Frankly, anything could have happened.

I got to work, plugging in my diagnostic reader as I paced around the walkway, looking for obvious wear and tear. But as I did so, I couldn't help but let out a sad laugh. I still couldn't believe they were trying to start some kind of exclusive community up here. Having built this incredibly complex machine, one that took hundreds of workers and generations of expertise, they wanted to choke off access to it. As if our situation weren't riding on a razor's edge, they wanted to introduce fresh scarcity — and bring back the old god: profit. But hadn't they learned anything? Thatcher had lied. There *was* a different way to live, there *was* an alternative. We'd *lived* it, scraping life from the bones of our fallen friends.

Maybe I was just starting to wax poetic in my old age, but I couldn't help but feel the metaphor in this machine. Humans were exactly the same, taking hundreds of parts to make us go, to allow life to cling to the planet. But you didn't see the fan telling the fuse box she was lesser. You didn't see the coolant trying to raise rents on the inverters. I knew I was just another part, but I was proud of that. I was here because someone else had kept me alive. And my work here today would probably save another life still.

I heard a beep from the diagnostics. I took a deep breath, squaring my shoulders as I walked back to the panel. I couldn't change the human condition. Hell, I could barely even manage to stay in one place. But today, I could fix this machine. I could keep these houses cold. And once I did…maybe they'd listen to me about who should live in them.

The Cabin

I was at the edge of the world, where life ended and death began. Behind me was my cabin: quaint, rustic — shockingly spared from the destruction — and ahead of me… The earth was scorched, the hills like a graveyard of ancient bones, the charred remains of tree trunks the only thing to interrupt the chalky earth.

They had sent me to find seeds, but it was slow, lonely work. The old pines, which were supposed to grow anew in the wake of a fire, had struggled to survive. The fires had been too close together, and the growing season after them too dry for anything to take root. Now, the government was starting over, trying to plant a new forest in the north, but they needed seeds. And perhaps, if they made someone like me look long enough, I'd find a pinecone or two they could use.

I put my pack on my shoulders and clipped on the hip belt, carefully adjusting the straps until the weight was balanced. Not that anything had changed in my pack… I carried the same kit into the forest each day, the same tools and the same amount of water. But it was a ritual, and one I needed. Maybe it was more of a superstition, like the old pro sports players from before who couldn't hit the ball without their shoes laced the right way. Either way, it was my own personal prayer to the forest, pleading that if I just showed enough care, proved I was worthy, the trees might offer up their treasure.

I could have used more water, of course, baking in the sun as I wandered the hills, but like everything else, my water was rationed. And for good reason. Many of the aquifers in the area had collapsed from overuse. Unfortunately, aquifers don't just refill like a jug. They're carefully constructed by time, pockets deep beneath the earth forced into the structure of the clay. And when they're emptied out? *Boom!* Collapsed, no more aquifer. Still, it was a miracle they'd found this one intact. I took my daily allotment with me into the forest — saving just enough to cook my meager rations after my shift — and it was a sort of life, hoping for enough rainfall to keep going but not so much the scarred hills wiped me off the map with a mudslide.

With everything set, I tapped the beam above the door, my ritual complete as I stepped off the porch. My boots crunched their way over a bed of brown pine needles, a sort of moat made of kindling separating my part of the forest from the other. And like every morning, it made me think of Quinn. We'd met in the Tree Corps, and the first time she'd kissed me had been on a bed of needles just like these. We'd taken our lunch under a tree, scooping the needles into a pile.

"It's our own private sofa," she'd joked, pulling me down beside her. "It's funny I can still enjoy things like this. This is another fire waiting to happen, but I can't help it."

I hadn't had anything particularly good to add. She was the clever one in the group, the eloquent one, but I'd smiled at least, and she'd seemed satisfied. It wasn't a *move,* my lack of words, but she'd always seemed convinced there were multitudes hiding behind my silence. I did think more thoughts than I said, didn't I? Maybe it was like scar tissue, covering over the person I'd been before. But would Quinn have liked the old me? Before the worst years, before I'd lost my family, I'd been talkative, hadn't I? Talkative-ish, anyway. For a while, it had felt like I never *stopped* talking, always boring someone half to death with my grad school anxieties.

"But if I did this program, then maybe I'd be qualified to—"

"No, I know, but my résumé can't compete with—"

"If only I hadn't been a teenager then. Who lets an eighteen-year-old pick a major that defines the rest of their life!"

But I suppose it was only natural to be anxious back then. There were a thousand fires burning in those days — both literal and figurative — growing ever larger on the horizon. Even as I droned away in the lab, desperate to make some kind of use of my botany, there hadn't been an obvious path. I'd specialized in lichens, and their habitat was evaporating before my eyes. How could I be useful against all that crisis?

In some ways, those voices had quieted after everything was lost. Suddenly, there was always something pressing and vital to do no matter what your skills, our collective descent down the hierarchy of needs suppressing my constant quest for meaning. More importantly, *Quinn* had given me meaning. Rebuilding the world had given me meaning. But now? Now there were choices to make again, and I felt paralyzed. Even this job hadn't seemed possible, but Quinn had pressed me to take it.

"I know we'll be apart for a while, but the way your eyes lit up, I can tell you want it."

But did I? What about all the other things I could be doing? What about my time with Quinn? They had still barely ramped up antibiotic production. What if I lost her to a cold, something she'd promise was only the sniffles while she volunteered for another night shift? If I wasn't hiking eighteen miles a day, I'm sure it would have made me sleepless with worry. But that was the problem with every job I'd ever had. *Someone* had to do it, but should that someone be me?

"If anyone can be in the woods alone for three months, it's you," Quinn had said. "No offense. I mean it in an endearing way."

And she had. She'd touched my arm and everything, making my heart drop into my feet. And she was right. I *was* good at being alone. Even if my mind was always churning with thoughts. Or maybe that was my secret? It reminded me of someone I'd worked with from before. They were incredibly efficient, perhaps *too* efficient, and they'd revealed to me one day that they had terrible OCD.

"Well," they'd said, laughing at my surprise — seeing as my anxious thoughts kept me from doing anything useful. "There's days I can't do anything at all, true, but when you grow up learning to multiply alongside your intrusive thoughts, you become a pretty good multitasker."

I guess we all went where we were suited. And even if I wanted to help with every single problem in the world, in the end, I could only work on one at a time. Besides, for as many useless mes as there were, there were probably a hundred Quinns, and they were getting us closer to something real, something good.

It was good to think and hike, of course, but like usual, I'd walked the first three miles in a trance, only realizing as I reached the top of the first rise. I stopped, putting down my bag to take a drink. I'd started calling this place Hornback Ridge. There were no accurate maps anymore — everything either burnt away or washed down the slope in a mudslide — but I'd gotten to know the area. And in a place this desolate, you had to make your own landmarks. Hornback Ridge was like a dragon's back, its knobby spine winding through the burnt forest.

I pulled my own makeshift map from my bag, looking at all the areas I could still search. I'd put X's through about half of them, starting each day at the ridge before fanning out in one direction or another. It was the highest point on my side of the mountains, and it kept me from getting lost.

I started to the west, the hours slipping by as I followed the slope of the hills. For a while, I was still in areas I'd at least scouted before, recognizing random boulders and trees along the way. But something that day pulled me farther. It could have just been the melancholy of thinking about Quinn — something that always made me walk farther than I should — but it just felt right. Even as I pushed toward the edge of my map, knowing I'd have to retrace whatever distance I walked to get back, I just kept going.

I walked all day, until the sun was more than halfway through the sky, when the ridge line just…ended. I stopped, looking down at a valley I'd never seen before. The mountains continued in the distance, but there was a gap about a quarter-mile wide nestled between the hills. I went up to the edge, tempted to reach for my pencil to mark it on the map, but something else caught my eye.

At the bottom of the valley was a giant cave. How had no one mentioned this before? It was angled downward like a drain in some god's bathtub, the eroding valley swirling toward it. More importantly, the soil was much darker. From the top of the ridge, I could see the change in color clearly. It was retaining moisture somehow, a miracle in its own right.

I started down the valley, forced to walk sideways so I could shuffle down the steep slope. But even as I worried I'd break my neck, I couldn't stop looking at that cave. I was tempted to slide my way down, but out here alone, a twisted ankle would end me just as easily as a mudslide. Still, before long, I reached the bottom, the soil seeming *bouncy* after so many months walking on ground as dry as bone. I stooped down, rolling some of it across my hand. I giggled like a kid, suddenly tempted to make a mud pie.

As I looked up, I locked eyes with the cave, the massive chasm drawing me in. The opening was some thirty feet wide, the rock just…torn away as the cavern disappeared into an inky blackness. I began walking toward it, uncaring for my lack of flashlights — I'd only go in a few yards, right? — when I stopped. There, on the ground, sprouting from the field of dark soil was a sapling. And surrounding it, pulled from the valley by the power of the drain, were hundreds of pinecones.

I fell to a seat, staring at the little tree. I'd found it. Or maybe, it had found me… Nature had found a way to answer the impossible question we'd posed to it: Can life push through the terrible things we've wrought? Apparently, it could.

"Thank you," I said, looking at the cave. "We don't deserve it, but thank you."

The Train

The train rumbled through the darkness, cold night air whooshing through my open window. In the dimmed night lights of the car, it felt like there was no distance between inside and out. I was part of the landscape even as I sped through it, the tree branches seeming to reach for me in the moonlight. A part of me wanted to reach back, to disappear into the night. It felt like a dream, like I'd left everything behind.

Unfortunately, moments like that are fleeting. They're essential, this sort of…distilling of the world's beauty, but reality always comes knocking again, demanding to be served. As much as I wanted to commune with the beauty of the universe, to enjoy the thrill of being on a train after so many years, I was still just one thing, one man. The air outside was chilly with fall, and sooner or later, someone would complain about my open window. So, I took one last deep breath of cold air and stood, shutting the window as I stretched.

We had hours to go yet, but I've never been any good at sleeping sitting up. Generally, I need a full night's sleep, and I was sure I'd pay for it in the morning, but I'd long ago dropped my anxiety around missed sleep. During the dark years, when things were at their worst, I'd usually spend two nights at a time pacing the halls with worry, only to sleep like the dead on the third night, finally paying off some of my sleep debt. And finally, I'd learned how to, if not thrive, at least survive without my rest.

I'd heard there would be sleeper cars on the new high-speed trains, but there was little chance of me affording one. Besides, even with how much the economy had recovered, were we really ready for differentiated tickets? I suppose someone must be making money out there, but there were enough of us still living on refugee credits I couldn't fathom how they'd fill the rooms. Still, I suppose luxuries of any kind were a good sign. Even if I couldn't afford them, it felt…freeing to know they were out there. If we had the resources for them, it meant the end was no longer so near.

It must be what it had felt like in the early 1900s when people first saw cars. There's a sort of wonder at the possibility of something new, even out of grasp, assuming, at least, that its magic might reach you eventually. Of course, the rampant inequality of the Gilded Age had bred the Bolshevik Revolution, but today, I decided to feel hopeful. Maybe we'd do things right this time. Maybe I'd be surprised. After all, even if it wasn't high-speed, I was on a train. Hell, I was on *vacation,* and that felt like a miracle.

I'd been in the Reconstruction Corps, of course, so I'd traveled, but this was different. I hadn't traveled for *fun* in fifteen years. In the corps, you stuck with your crew, herded like cattle from one site to another, with only more desolation waiting for you on the other side. This trip was entirely mine, a blank page, a map with no edges. Even with an itinerary and a ticket paid for months ago, there was something about traveling alone that felt like anything could happen.

I went into the dining car, where there were still a half-dozen people milling about. There were a few couples, all in their own quiet conversations, heads bowed together, with a few stragglers sitting at the bar. Even though the bartender was dressed no differently from me — standard issue recycled wool pants and a hand-sewn shirt — he had the look of a professional about him, his sleeves rolled up and a towel over one shoulder. He didn't move from the back of the bar, his arms folded before him, but he smiled warmly, nodding his head toward an open stool.

I sat, the cushion oddly comfortable. It looked like leather — salvage, perhaps? Unless those leather cloning facilities were already operational, though it seemed a bit…wasteful, even on vacation.

"What can I get you?" the bartender asked.

"I…don't know," I said, suddenly paralyzed by the array of bottles and jars behind him. It wasn't just a bar, there were snacks and things, but that didn't make it any less overwhelming. Each bottle was a glowing gem, and I some wayward robber who'd gotten into the vault.

"First vacation?" the bartender asked gently.

"Is it obvious?"

"Not terribly, no," he said, reaching for a bound menu. "But everyone goes through it. It's just been too long for most of us. Here, this usually works."

He flipped to the back of the menu, his movements precise as he found the page, turning it toward me. I picked it up, staring at the hand-drawn image of a bowl, a mountain of color rising from its top.

"Ice cream?" I asked, his smile widening at the shocked look on my face. "Like, real ice cream?"

"Well, define real," he said, leaning to open a freezer by his knees. "It's kelp-based, but after all these years, I can hardly remember the difference myself. It's not bad, and we actually have more than one flavor."

I forced my mouth closed, wiping it absently — even if the drool was only in my head.

"How many credits is that, though? I only have so many for the trip and…"

The bartender raised his hand, cutting me off.

"Comes with the price of the ticket," he said. "You get one snack, one drink, and breakfast in the morning before we arrive — though they'll bring that around on the cart. So, what flavor?"

They were written on the carton in what had to be the bartender's curling hand. Strawberry, vanilla, and chocolate. It would have been so basic *before*, but now, seeing chocolate alone was incredible. I'd finally gotten used to coffee being back — ignoring all the complex physics of international trade that went over my head — but an entire carton of chocolate ice cream? It was baffling.

"Strawberry," I said before I could change my mind. I might regret not saying chocolate later, but it felt like a bridge too far, like I might wake up from my dream if I flew too close to the sun. Besides, there was always the train ride back, wasn't there?

"Hmm," the bartender hummed, nodding to himself as he pulled one of the cartons out. Was he surprised by my choice? Did I not look like a strawberry man? Either way, I was too mesmerized to care as I watched him place a perfect sphere of strawberry in a beautiful glass dish.

"Anything to drink?" he asked as he placed it in front of me, a dainty little spoon lodged into the side of the strawberry mountain.

Now my mouth was dry, and I had to unstick my tongue.

"Umm, no," I said. "This is good."

"Water?" he asked, pointing with his thumb at a large green tank at the end of the bar. How long had it been since someone casually offered me water in a restaurant? Twenty years?

He followed my eyes, chuckling.

"I'm sorry, I didn't think I'd be blowing your mind so much. Seriously, we have plenty. The train runs on hydrogen and this filters in from the fuel cells. The cell is ceramic too, so it's fine to drink."

"Oh, well…a glass of water, then. Thank you."

He placed an equally perfect drinking glass in front of me with a nod. Then, his job guiding a clueless traveler done, he retreated to the other end of the bar.

I didn't want to let the ice cream melt — was actually terrified I'd somehow ruin the experience for myself — but the water was just as captivating. It filled the glass like a tiny ocean, taking on a golden hue in the candlelight. I reached for it, taking a slow, careful sip. I thought it might somehow taste like an engine, but it was perfect — cold and clean, like it had melted from an icicle.

"Incredible," I said to myself, though thankfully no one at the bar looked my way. I'm sure they'd all been through this dance before. I started in on the ice cream, no longer able to delay in good conscience. As I took my first bite, the train went through another town, its whistle calling through the night. And for the first time, it really dawned on me. I was alive. I was on vacation. I was eating ice cream. Perhaps I didn't need to distill the world's beauty. Perhaps I was living that beauty, a whole universe distilled into a single glass bowl. And for some reason, the universe tasted like strawberries.

School

I stopped to fix my ponytail, the rough denim tie having come loose while I was lying on my back to fix the electrical cable. The old schoolroom was blazingly hot, the sun glaring through the blinds, each piece of dust lighting up like it might catch fire. I was much too old to be lying on the ground staring up at a bunch of wires, but still, I had a goofy smile on my face. It was…bliss. I loved my work, and lately, I'd been feeling happier than I had in ages. Most importantly, with the sort of magic particular to older women, no one could take my joy away from me anymore.

When I was young, I'd been obsessed with becoming an electrician. Well, not *young,* but certainly younger. I was in my thirties, which seems impossibly young now after everything I've been through, but too deep into my life as an office worker to change course. Still, I'd sit up late at night on my laptop, watching videos on wiring and looking up courses I'd never end up taking. I could have dropped everything and gone to trade school, I suppose, but I don't think my obsession was about *being* an electrician. It was about not feeling so *useless.*

That was the great irony of our highly specialized economy, wasn't it? Supposedly, the market was supposed to clear, supply and demand putting all the little workers in their most useful categories. But in reality — like with all economic models — there were frictions.

You went to school, or tried to, picking some major out of a hat. You studied as hard as you could, and then, invariably, you discovered that there were no jobs for that particular thing. So, you found whatever job you could and then spent thousands of more hours on grad school or certifications — or both — just to stave off the precarity of losing what little hold you had on a middle-class life. Before everything fell apart, to not have money was to die a death of despair. It wasn't any more tragic than the millions of deaths we saw after, but it was more…offensive somehow, more ridiculous for how unnecessary it was. *Look,* we collectively seemed to say, *we have plenty of food, but you can't have any.*

To me, modern work — at a corporation, anyway — had always felt like a giant boat. Everybody went to their own part of the ship every morning, unseen until the whistle sounded at the end of your shift. You weren't sure what everybody did, but as long as the boat kept floating, everybody got paid. Sometimes, the big boss would throw some people overboard — something about keeping the bilge fresh — but you just kept humming along. Some jobs were probably literally vital, like tying the ropes down, but my jobs had always wound up being more like mopping the decks. Important enough, but it didn't necessarily keep the whole thing moving.

So, anyway, my obsession. The thing was, I had always been a pretty handy person. In spite of the mountain of sexism in our culture — and my dad's fervent wish for a boy — he'd had me. He'd had his own shipping route back then, with a fleet of cars he drove all around Illinois delivering packages — which seems almost quaint now that I'm back to walking a mile every morning for water… Anyway, he taught me all about tools and how things worked. We replaced the oil in his vans, changed the tires, kept everything running in the house, too. But, like many wise do-it-yourselfers, we never touched the electric. My grandfather never had, either.

"There's zaps you never forget," he used to say, "and zaps you never wake up from. Best not to find out the difference."

I'd grown up in the part of the 2000s where college still seemed mandatory — or rational, even — and I followed the track laid out for me. I eventually ended up as an energy analyst, ironically enough, tracking electricity on spreadsheets, which was…interesting if not spiritually soothing for my many existential aches. Eventually, when we were desperately trying to transition to clean energy before things fell apart, we kept talking about how we needed more electricians to electrify everything. So, I started my constant dreaming, even if nothing ever came of it.

But it doesn't end at electricians, does it? Just like doomsday preppers — whose fates turned out…*predictably* with the very planet falling apart around us — just being an electrician doesn't solve for the fact that we need every single person to make society go. Electricians still need quality cables, not to mention tools, and running electricity into a house implies there's electricity to be run. Before, that took a whole fleet of workers and engineers to ensure the grid was stable and ready at the call of a light switch. The whole thing was baffling if you really thought about it, like science fiction, traveling our wires at 300,000 kilometers per second, the wavelength longer than you could drive in three days.

Satisfied by my work on the wires, I groaned as I finally sat up, pulling myself up to my desk as I sat, looking at the dozens of books I had spread out on the desk. A lot of them talked about discoveries made in the 1800s, a sort of technological backstep we'd been forced to make. Even if we knew a lot more about the *why* of electricity, people like Michael Faraday had certainly known a lot more about the how — at least compared to a regular person like me. There were clearly still electrical engineers living, but they'd almost all been gobbled up by the Corps, working on building up the country again. Maybe they'd make it to our little town eventually, but I didn't wanna bet on living long enough to find out.

Studying the diagram one last time, I took a magnet from the work bench, affixing it to the rotor of the new engine we were building. We'd stripped the parts from old cars — especially the older electric ones that had still used rare earth magnets before they changed them out in the mid-2020s. What the engine would be used for was anyone's guess at that point, but no one at the school seemed to mind its lack of purpose either. We were finally back to the core of humanity, experimenting for experiment's sake and hoping we could make life just an ounce better when we were through. We had dozens of farms outside town eager for any sliver of technology, and we might finally deliver it to them.

With the magnet in place, I swiveled to turn on the flow of electricity. It was a hodgepodge of a machine, to say the least, but if it worked, it was the start of something — and in it, the way I'd finally found to be useful. I'd been an analyst my whole working life, someone who was meant to distill tough concepts into eager minds. And now I really could — and not just for some insidious hunger for profit, either. Our town had started an engineering school, and I was one of the old fogies lucky enough to do lesson planning.

As the current entered the machine, it began to whir, an alternating current — thanks to the inverters we'd found with the old solar panels — creating alternating fields between the rotor and the stator. And it...*began to spin*. I laughed, clapping as I did a little dance. It reminded me of the biography of Tesla I'd been reading. He claimed to have made one of his greatest discoveries while wandering the streets with his friend reciting Goethe. I hadn't had access to the internet — or what was left of it — in years, but we had raided the public library. And as silly as it felt, I grabbed the book of poems I'd borrowed, opening to the page I'd marked.

"The glow retreats," I read aloud to the empty room, "done is the day of toil; It yonder hastes, new fields of life exploring; Ah, that no wing can lift me from the soil, Upon its track to follow, follow soaring!"

Even if I was still a nobody, I was a fragment of a billion somebodies, the great expanse of humanity who'd discovered electricity — and was discovering it again. Even after everything we'd suffered through our own hubris, we could start fresh, a little humbler, a little more open, and hopefully, a whole lot happier.

Islands

My hands were tight against the wheel, the jib lowered so I could see as we pushed north along the Chicago River. The deck was near to bursting with crates of blueberries, our entire crop, and I wasn't about to crash within a mile of North Market. Maybe I shouldn't have been using the sail, but after four days on Lake Michigan — only occasionally downwind — our backup propulsion was lower on hydrogen than I'd have liked. By some miracle, we actually had an old mini-electrolyzer, though that would require getting home a day late. So, sail it was. Still, it was early, and the river was quiet — at least as far as traffic was concerned.

To my right, there was a splash, the sound of a muskrat jumping in the water. I looked, though the water was already smooth again, a pair of cranes the only thing to see as they looked back at me from the banks.

"Sure we shouldn't bring one back with us?" Francie asked, smiling from the front of the boat. "There'll be room after we drop the crates."

I laughed.

"I'm not stopping you, though I think the muskrat would have an issue with it."

"You're right," she said with a wink, "we'll have to bring his friends too."

Francie had to be the biggest vermin lover on earth — and I truly don't mean that in a derogatory sense. She adored small mammals — of every kind — and had successfully saved and raised two mice already in the winters we'd been at the farm. She'd also somehow bonded with the local raccoons, a dozen of them emerging every morning while she drank her coffee. It almost made you think she went out there with a flute or something. But the promise of muskrats — their population reportedly surging as pollution on the river fell — had made her sign up for this second summer shipment. That was all fine by me, of course. She was an incredible sailor, well worth the risk of a furry stowaway.

"No pets," Brian said, coming from below deck with a grin, a coffee in his hand. I still hadn't had the courage to touch the stuff, afraid I'd just get addicted again after all the years they couldn't import it. Still, the smell was incredible.

"Don't pretend you haven't made me say this a thousand times," Francie said, rolling her eyes. "They're not *pets,* dad. If anything, they're mascots, totems — *gods,* even — proof that even if we destroyed ourselves, we couldn't destroy *life.*"

"I know, love," he said, laughing as he sat across from her. He looked at me, gesturing with his coffee. "How about you, captain?"

"I just move the berries," I said, chuckling.

Still, I think I did sort of know what she meant. Francie might accidentally wind up starting her own cult someday, but who could blame her? The old ways had let us down. I personally still held to my own sort of Christianity, but it was the open-minded kind. I'd always been on the liberal edges of Christendom anyway, so why couldn't that include a girl who called to raccoons? After all, what was the point of imperialist Christianity without an empire? All the misplaced beliefs of my grandfather about 'dominion' and owning the earth had really just been cover anyway, a mask for colonialism and every other capitalist impulse we'd used to pillage since the Roman Empire. We'd dominated the earth, alright, but we'd destroyed it, too.

Francie's main point, though, that life remained, certainly seemed true now, even if I wouldn't have believed her two years ago. But now, even with all we'd lost, I'd never been happier. I had nothing — not even a single family member like Francie did, her dad never leaving her side — but I was part of something all the same. And on the farm, with dozens of little families around me, I belonged.

No man is an island. We'd said that so casually before everything fell apart, even if we'd done our best to do the opposite. If anything, we'd turned ourselves into archipelagos, little chains of islands barely strung together, our supplies airdropped from above. Now, of course, I could see we'd all been in a death spiral without realizing it, buying things to numb the pain and staying in horrible jobs to pay for them. You still had to volunteer in your spare time, of course, just to stomach all the awfulness we'd wrought, but that only led to burnout — and whatever dopamine rush was close at hand to push it back. In the end, outside of the one or two nights a week you got to spend with friends, we were completely and utterly alone.

But my life now, however precarious, was *whole.* I strove every day to do something great, to feed people, all while reconnecting with the earth, doing things in a way that wasn't leaching the life from the soil. And meanwhile, I got to spend those days with people who cared for me, and I got to care for them. I wasn't desperately jamming in volunteer hours because I could spend them on the farm, picking wildflowers for Jan or fixing the shed. And at the end of the day, we got to gather around a fire and just...*be.* Brian ribbing Francie, Jerri singing some song only half of us remembered. It was incredible, and it was *alive.* Wasn't that what God wanted for us?

"How about a turtle?" I suggested, nodding toward a giant shelled monstrosity on a nearby log, out early before the sun. It reminded me of Chonkosaurus, the behemoth the news had covered so extensively when I'd lived in Chicago twenty years earlier. Maybe this was Son of Chonkosaurus, carrying on the family legacy as he snapped his way through life.

"You got small fingers," Brian said, pointing at Francie's hands, "maybe he won't grab any."

"Har-har," she said. "But I think we have enough dinosaurs in the family."

"I'm your dad's age, you know," I said in protest.

"Sure," she said, "but his are in dog years."

Up ahead, the market appeared on the other side of the Lawrence Avenue bridge, the white cloth of the tents visible in the shadow of the old pumping station. Already there was smoke from fires roasting all manner of things, and soon the place would be full of people. Hopefully, we'd get to try something new, but even the food was nothing compared to the looks on everyone's faces when we arrived. Illinois and its loamy soil were terrible for blueberries, but with the weather finally stabilizing and Michigan's ancient limestone, we were about to rain blue on their unsuspecting heads.

I trimmed the sail, Francie popping up to grab our ties. Maybe I was Brian's age, but I felt *new*. Each day now was like a hundred before, time finally distilling to its essence. Maybe I wasn't as free as a muskrat, but I was alive. Maybe the opposite of an island wasn't a landmass but a boat. Someone who was willing to brave the water to find everyone else, even if all they brought with them was blueberries.

On Batteries and Garbage

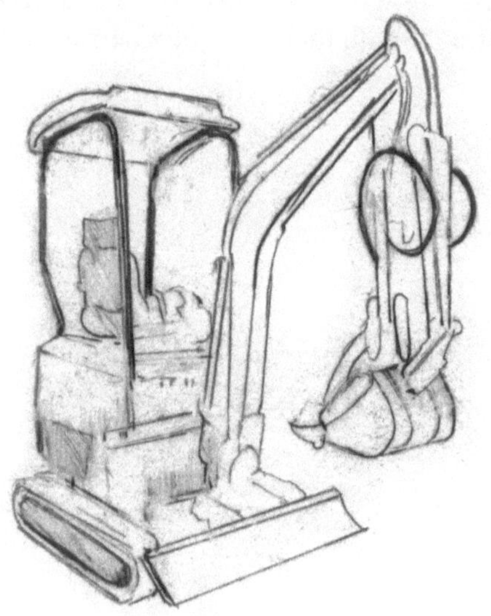

I shook my right hand back and forth, trying to keep the cramp at bay as I switched to my left. I started the crank again, the pulleys spinning as the stone moved higher. I'd been at it for twenty minutes already, but it was only three feet off the ground. On any other day, maybe that would have felt impressive — it was a three-ton block the size of a car, after all — but for the first time in months, I was alone at the worksite. I'd get it off the ground eventually, but without Gemma, I felt like Sisyphus.

Finally, after another twenty minutes — my arms somewhere between jelly and rubber — the block passed the yellow flag, marking at least an hour of electric power. That would have to do. I flipped the switch on the fuse box, the pulley suddenly spinning the other way as the stone began its slow descent. The box's light turned on, and the electric meter sprang to life, its dial rising from the dead.

For probably the hundredth time since I started the project, I thought how much better winding the pulleys would be with a bike attached to the crank. Unfortunately, I knew the higher-ups would say they 'couldn't spare it.' Just like every other thing in this zone. There were too many 'strategic priorities' elsewhere, I guess, and protecting groundwater simply didn't matter when you had buckets of the stuff still raining on you from the sky. And for what had to be the thousandth time that morning, I heard Gemma's voice in my head:

"I told you we shouldn't have come here."

She didn't sound judgmental or self-righteous, just…defeated. She had never been happy to be proven right, but I had brought her here, and now she was gone, unable to pull me back from a pit I'd dug for myself. And the worst part was, I knew she was right. But for some reason, I stayed on. I couldn't take another failure. The losing, the dying, the scraping, those were supposed to be over. And even if I got buried in this trash heap, I wasn't giving up here, refusing to cross that final line in the sand.

I walked over to my computer, the screen flickering on now that the battery was running again. I cracked my knuckles impatiently as it powered on, running through its launch files. The thing was ancient, from the '20s — like most computers — though at least it was reliable enough. It took forever to boot up and even longer to execute the code, but it hadn't failed me yet. Though the thought suddenly put a fresh knot in my stomach… If the computer ever gave out, the section director most certainly wouldn't ever give me another. He'd barely given me this one, and that was only after I'd proved I could get it working again.

"You're like hunting for treasure in reverse."

Gemma's voice again, this time from years ago, when we'd first met. She'd admired me then, even if my failures were already piling up around me like rusted armor. But for the first time in my life, someone had understood. Understood why I couldn't let go of this obsession. Understood why after the water was poisoned in my town, I couldn't let it happen again.

Finally launching a command prompt, I typed in the sequence code.

Written in Python 3 of all things, I'd memorized the prompt, typing it perfectly on my first try despite the aching in my knuckles. As the code ran, the scanner turned on, whirring as it bleeped radar scans into the hillside. Blips began to appear on the screen, little pockets where something hollow might be. Unfortunately, there were hundreds, and every day I had to pick just one to excavate. Like finding a needle in a needlestack.

A group of seagulls flew by, crying as they looked for food. Even as the hillside turned from trash back into grass, apparently they remembered the landfill. I'd read somewhere once that seagulls could live thirty years — which was a weirdly scary thought for some reason — but maybe there were elder gulls out there still talking about the glory days. Which wasn't so different from humans, not that those times had really been all that glorious…

There was bounty, sure — however illusory — and I'd occasionally had a good time. But when I think about the old times now, I can only picture corporate town halls. Even though no one ever said anything even remotely useful, they're lodged in my head. I know strong emotions can lay down new neurons, so maybe it was just my rage from drowning in corporate doublespeak, but it's all just buried in my mind.

"We're thinking long AND short-term."

"We have a good partnership with the board, which is why we're probably only going to withhold bonuses for one year instead of two."

"You need to take an ownership mindset (about this business that we one hundred percent control and you do not)."

So maybe there was some subtext in my memories, but something about all that lying had always lit a fire in me. They say anger is your greatest champion, so I guess I'm grateful. Maybe my champion didn't win me any battles, but it sure ensured I wouldn't ever give up the war. Even now, looking for a cache of toxic waste my corporation had dumped, I was fighting on.

I picked one of the blips at random, heading for my excavator. When Gemma was still here, I would have made up a reason why that blip was the best.

"See how it tilts to the side? See how the blob on the radar screen is extra blobby? That feels unnatural."

But I was alone now, and since I could finally be honest with myself, I didn't have a reason. After trying hundreds of hunches, I simply didn't know what to believe anymore. I certainly couldn't believe in myself. My mind was too split, an empty basin divided by an impenetrable wall of doubt.

The excavator was a sort of Frankenstein situation, a hulking thing made from a modified bulldozer from before. It was stored under an open-air shed, and it was rusting on basically all sides where its old yellow paint had worn off. Still, I was happy to have it. And more importantly, with its tiny modified digging arm on the front, it would hopefully avoid leaking the contents of the waste I was trying so hard to find.

I climbed into the seat, clicking on the battery to see how much hydrogen I had left in the tank. About half. I looked over at the large liquified hydrogen tank the higher-ups had given me. There was probably enough left to fill the tank five more times, which gave me, what…a month? When the hydrogen ran out, I was done. I suppose I could try to excavate by hand, but there were things in the landfill a shovel wouldn't get through. Besides, the purifier on the tailpipe of the excavator was the only water source they'd given me, which maybe said all I needed to know about the value of my little project…

The excavator roared to life, and I eased the clutch, rumbling across the uneven ground toward the blip on the radar. I'd rigged a map reader to run remotely off my software, though it would die as soon as the crank battery ran out. Still, the landfill was only fifty acres, and even at the slow walking speed of the excavator, I would find it well before the juice ran out.

Winding through the site, it felt like some kind of archaeological dig, the grassy hillside open in random places, the soil littered with piles of plastic and metal. I'd promised myself I'd save the last tank of hydrogen for cleanup, of course, but a few piles of trash weren't all that concerning compared to the toxins I was looking for. Still, now that humanity's demise wasn't so certain — something I certainly hadn't always been so confident of in the hard years — it was interesting to think of what would become of this place. In one spot, there was a stack of children's toys, the fading rainbow-colored plastic surrounded by wildflowers. Even as destructive as this place had been, in a uniquely human way, it was sort of beautiful too.

Finally, I reached the radar blip, the screen next to the wheel chirping at me. I got down from the excavator, looking at…*nothing*. I was used to this part, of course, but with the pressure building to succeed, it felt more daunting than it had in a while. Like always, though, my job was to somehow turn a hillside into a discovery, literally turning trash into misguided treasure.

I started with my sounding pole, sticking it through the soil at random intervals to make sure there wasn't anything near the surface. The toxins

I was looking for should be stored in drums sealed in concrete, but who knew if that was true? The last thing I wanted was to pierce their casing with the excavator. If I did that, I'd be covered in the stuff before I had a chance to scream.

Satisfied, I got back in the excavator, carving into the hillside with long, clean strokes. Once I had a sort of half-octagon shape, I took a hand shovel, slowly knocking dirt off the sides to see what I could reveal. Every so often, the columns of dirt would cave, revealing pockets of inorganic material: plastic tubs, bottles, a metal colander. No matter what spilled out, though, I kept at it, kicking the plastic into a pile so I could—

There was something there.

I threw down my shovel, patting my vest pockets for my brush. Gemma used to make fun of me for that, a luxury that took my archeological pretense just a bit too far. But that day, I was grateful. There was something hard right in the middle of the mound, and now I could get the dirt off without scraping whatever it was.

I swept in broad strokes, slowly revealing what looked like a concrete block. Unable to contain my excitement, I went faster, my wrist starting to ache as I furiously swept the brush back and forth. Finally, on my third pass, I found a spot that was darker than the others, what looked like a metal plate affixed to the concrete.

I splashed a little water on it, finding my old company's name imprinted into the plate.

My hand went for my phone, my brain still hardwired to reach for Gemma. She would be happy for me, sure, but would it change anything? After all, she hadn't left because I couldn't find what I was looking for. She'd left because I couldn't see what was right in front of me. The time to reach out for her was in the past, a hundred opportunities burnt on the altar of my obsession.

I ran a hand through my hair, letting out a deep sigh. It was alright. Wherever she was in the city, at least she'd be drinking safer water. I took out my phone, dialing the station chief. He might screen my call, certainly didn't care whether I lived or died, but he'd want to hear about this, proof he'd finally gotten a return on his investment.

"Hey, Chief? Yeah, I found it."

Mending

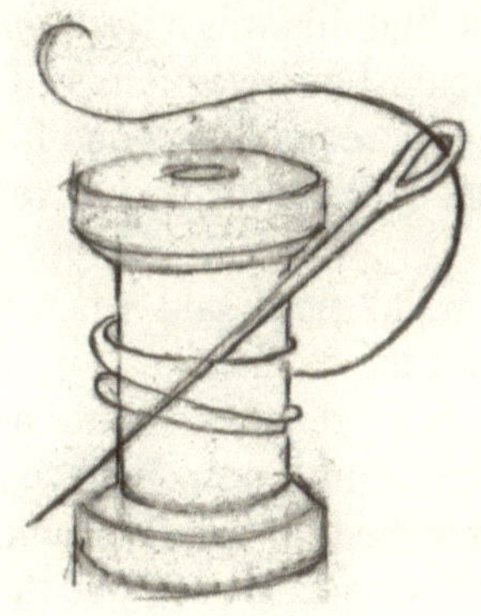

I looked again at the buttons arranged on my sewing table. There were ten in all, each one a different shape and color, like tiny planets waiting to be explored. In short, they were marvelous. Not that it helped me get any closer to a decision. Still, I had time. They weren't due to be picked up until closing time, and with all my easy jobs out of the way, it meant I could obsess.

I rested my head on my hands, trying to imagine my customer going through his day. He was in the Tree Corps, working out of the Foster Street substation just west of the water line. I imagined him at work, his arms reaching above his head to prune a branch, bending over to plant a seed. Not that I'd want to be accused of daydreaming about a strapping young forester. Don't get me wrong, he was handsome enough, but I'm a woman of the cloth first, and my imagination was reserved only for the shirt I was trying to repair.

I lifted my head, running my finger along the tear in the fabric. The shirt had opened up along a seam behind the shoulder, the left arm threatening to separate from the rest. I would mend that, of course, but I needed the piece to function as a whole. The corps uniforms were designed with a little give added along the seams, so I'd let it out, but *truly* fixing it started with the buttons.

The buttons he had now were standard issue, but they were pulling on their eyelets, no longer the right fit for the shirt. And once I let the shirt out, if I didn't fix them, it would pinch and sag in odd places. Comfort was important, of course, but this was a *uniform,* a suit of armor for this man's righteous battle against our own demise. I wanted him to be proud of his uniform, but even more, every second he wasn't forced to waste thinking about his bunchy buttons was a moment he could spend thinking about trees.

"I heard you're the best," he'd said when he brought the shirt in, handing it reverently over the counter.

Most people had gotten good enough to do their own simple mending at home, but this was no simple job. In fact, I could see when he'd walked in where he'd patched his pants around the left knee. But this was his uniform shirt; a special case, and one that deserved special care. I'm not so sure about being the best, but I knew then I'd have no choice but to give it my all.

When we were younger, before things fell apart, my friends thought I was so quirky for sewing my own clothes. I was like some kind of extinct fish, swimming in a sea of fast fashion. And sure, I'm quirky enough, but mostly I think I was just *stubborn,* refusing to give up when everyone else told me to throw something away.

In fact, I can remember the moment my obsession was born. It was well before things completely fell apart — the mid-20s maybe? — and there was a pair of pants I adored, wearing them way more than should have been socially acceptable. But I had been working from home at the time, and I was in my sweatpants era. Still, these sweatpants were tapered, and they made me look like I was only sixty percent goblin.

They had nice pockets and a tweed-like thread on the outside that made them almost stylish if you saw me from far away.

Maybe *adore* isn't the right word. Adore implies a type of love, and I'm not sure I gave those pants any love in return for all their service. Not like I would do now, repairing and mending them in return for all they did. I was obsessed, true. Dependent? Definitely. But I didn't adore those pants, I *smothered* them, wearing them until a tear appeared in the crotch.

I ignored it at first, even then trying to abstain from the horrors of fast fashion. I was attempting to slow down time, to eke out the precious minutes I had left with my poor pants. Unfortunately, back then, I lacked the skills to do anything else about it, so the tear grew, spreading until it was beyond my control. Finally, I swallowed my pride and went to a tailor. I may look like a creature of the night arriving with my imperfect trousers, but it seemed better to pay for repairs than to give up altogether. Surely the tailor down the street would want the business too, right?

He did not.

I watched as the old Greek man put on his glasses, poking and prodding my wicked handiwork.

"Dead," he finally said, his accent heavy.

"Excuse me?" I asked, thinking I'd misunderstood.

"You know alive?" he asked, shaking the pants for emphasis. "Alive, dead. These dead. Just buy new."

"Right," I said, feeling the shame creep into my stomach. "It's just, I don't want to buy new. I want to save these, save the resources."

"Save?" he asked, shaking his head at who he thought was clearly a cheapskate. "How much new cost?"

"I don't know," I stammered, "sixty? But it's not about the money."

"This cost one hundred to fix. I do, but very bad for you. You must find this fabric, too. Bring me fabric, I fix. One hundred."

I hadn't even considered the semi-stylish tweed-like exterior of the pants. I had honestly been so prepared to sacrifice for this repair that I'd assumed he'd just use any old gray fabric, the mismatch hidden by my thighs — which was at least marginally better than a clear shot of my knickers while I was walking.

So, I left in shame, not even returning anymore for dry cleaning lest he recognize me as his Dead Pants Penelope. But staring at my broken pants in the laundry hamper the next day, I felt a surge of…*something*. Rage, maybe? Either way, I felt a deep desire to act. It was like the pants were calling out for help — though I luckily hadn't started hearing voices — and as much as I hated myself for my late-stage capitalistic uselessness, for once, I took action and signed up for a sewing class.

Not that my shame ended there, of course, but this time I was ready. When the other women in the class announced what their final project would be, they almost all said they wanted to make their own clothes.

"I want something that fits my style," one said.

"I love to thrift, but nothing ever fits me," said another.

"I have my sister's wedding coming up, and I want something unique."

When they got to me, I almost lied, but I could see my busted pants staring at me from my bag, and I knew I had to speak my truth.

"I want to fix my pants," I said proudly — and perhaps a bit too loudly. The instructor raised an eyebrow.

"You signed up for a twenty-week sewing class to…fix some pants?"

"That is correct," I said, the silence suddenly deafening. But then, something shifted.

"Well, heck yeah!" she said. "We can do that! No point in making your own clothes if you can't fix 'em, too, right, ladies?"

And here I am, my quirks suddenly vital. Fast fashion, like every other environmental depravity we performed, couldn't support its own weight. The old economics used to write off externalities, as if Mother Nature was some third party to our system.

"More is always better," an economics professor said to me in undergrad as he drew the supply and demand functions I was forced to burn into my brain. "And cheaper is always more."

But, of course, it wasn't: labor conditions, human rights violations, materials that leached the earth. They weren't giving us a deal, they were taking our very life force until nothing was left, until my friend in the Tree Corps could only get two shirts to use while he saved what was left of the planet. Fortunately, I'd learned long before that there was another way. More may be better, but *enough* was best. And with a little love — a sort of externality of the soul — I could make something incredible.

I picked up a button, its tortoiseshell pattern suddenly calling to me, begging to be sorted from the rest. I rolled it between my thumb and index finger, and I could *feel* how right it was. It would bring balance to the shirt, realigning the fit. Not too snug, but not too loose, either. Just a bit smaller than his old buttons, but big enough to hold the shirt closed. More importantly, it would give him something unique, something that said, "I'm the one with the trees!"

So, I picked up my little treasure and set it on the shirt. It was time to sew.

63% Coverage

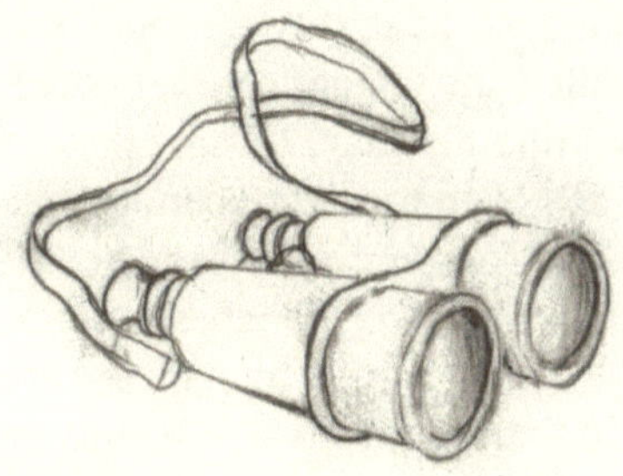

Twenty-two degrees. That's how much they said bare concrete used to heat up the city. It's terrifying to think about now, after everything that happened, but it feels distant too, almost unreal. From the observation tower, watching the trees sway in the wind, their leaves blending with the grass of green roofs, it felt like a story you might tell to scare kids. Not that I'll ever forget how real and awful all that heat was…

Still, it feels different when you can do something about it. And in that moment, I knew I could, even if I was only pushing us over the finish line. 63%. A goal that had felt so far away for so long. But we were almost there, just two percentage points shy of finishing the urban canopy in Chicago. They said the city used to only have around fifteen percent. That was before, of course, when no one seemed to hear the ecological freight train bearing down on them.

I can barely remember being a child, but I strangely remember there being a lot of trees. The shade in the summer, the odd-shaped crab apple tree in my parents backyard. Ravenswood had been like a Garden of Eden, each yard a tiny preservation. We obviously needed somewhere for the animals to be at peace, but looking back, it's hard to ignore the fact that those yards hadn't been curated for biodiversity but for the million-dollar homes sitting on them. Like everything in the city back then, it left things unequal, even shade itself.

We've seen the old maps, and they're abysmal, damning even. On the south side — where the wealthy and white had already spent a century redlining property values into oblivion — the canopy numbers were even lower, with some neighborhoods only getting ten percent coverage. Even with the heat shelters, heat waves would kill people every year, landlords neglecting rules, the concrete baking the houses like a kiln.

With all that in my mind that day, I found myself stretching, looking just a little bit harder as I tried to fill the canopy. That was no easy task, by the way. Trees aren't like aluminum cans, ready to stack on a shelf. They need room — for roots, for branches — enough to capture what they need. And they also need care, which meant around a quarter of the corps — myself included, hopefully — would be staying behind in Chicago to make sure the trees got everything they needed.

Still, I've always loved that about plants. We get so lost in bipedalism, bilateral symmetry — all the things that make us human — that we forget about the alternative. Plants embrace the spherical, branching out as they form bulbs and blossoms, nature's perfect shapes for taking in all the solar system has to offer. Unfortunately, while they could communicate, they couldn't move, couldn't protect themselves or plan for our destruction. Now, as we tried again, we just had to give them a chance.

As I scanned the canopy again, I finally spotted a gap, the triangle of shadow between the other trees a telltale sign of a hole in the leaves. I'd have to go down and check, of course. Some of the holes were wire hubs, a place for maintenance crews to plug in and check on the microgrids. We could plant bushes or prairie grass there, of course — and probably had — but it was always worth having a look. Our maps were getting pretty good, especially once we'd switched the streetlamp LEDs from light poles to tree attachments. But when the map was so beautifully covered in green, sometimes you had to see for yourself.

I climbed down the ladder, savoring the cool air as I dipped below the canopy. It felt like being in a submarine, diving below the surface into the cool dark of the ocean. There was even a slight breeze, the temperature differential on the surface always good for a bit of fresh air. Getting on my corps-issued bike, I quickly crossed the blocks as I held onto the location of that spot in my mind. The sun was up, and people were out and about, a few waving as they passed, recognizing my uniform.

Our work hadn't always been an easy sell, of course. Many understood the purpose, especially when we explained to them how much it would cool their homes. Still, there were times, especially in the beginning, when it had grated on people. In the end, it's eminent domain, just the kind where we don't tear your house down and try to leave it cooler and a bit prettier…

Finally, I reached 44th Street, thinking I'd missed it. I slowed, looking to my right when I saw the light, like some kind of heavenly beam breaking through the clouds. I walked toward it, taking a path through the prairie grass they'd set up along the road. There was a beautiful black walnut by the clearing, but it was otherwise well and truly open.

I went and sat on the blank patch of grass, stretching my arms in the air as I tried to imagine what it would feel like to be the sapling we planted there, stretching toward the sun. I tilted my head back, letting the light shine on my face, warming the back of my neck where the dark green of my uniform soaked up its rays.

Finally, I stood, marking the place on my pocket map. But before I radioed, I went over to the walnut tree, putting my forehead to its bark.

"I hope you don't mind," I said, "but we're going to get you a little friend. Keep an eye on them, okay?"

It didn't answer, of course, but I was sure it could hear me all the same. After all, every bit of research over the years had pointed to plants basically having thoughts, even if they didn't look like ours. And that was a good thing. Even though it was respectful to ask, I knew this tree would embrace its neighbor. After all, if love was supposed to be patient and kind, who was more patient than a tree? They watched us live and die, living hundreds of years when we let them, bearing witness to the world on the banks of time's mighty river.

I patted the bark one last time, reaching for my radio. This would be a good spot. And some day, when the canopy was taller than the skyscrapers downtown, we could all rest in the shade.

Strawberries

I put one last coat of red paint on the rock, rolling it to the ground with the others. I looked over my shoulder, looking to see if the crows were watching me from the tree line. Would my gambit work again? They were fiercely intelligent, likely the most admirable adversaries I'd ever faced, and I kept thinking my tricks would stop working. I hoped they could sense my respect, of course — I grew a patch of wild corn exclusively for them. But as tasty as corn was, it couldn't hold a candle to my strawberries. And with all the changes we'd made, we needed this crop, needed the crows to leave something for the people.

I could see my wife on the porch, laughing at me from the farmhouse. She always thought my rock painting was a bit ridiculous — even on the year she finally admitted it worked. This year, though, she thought it was particularly silly. And it may well be. In years past, we'd had acres of strawberries to protect, but now, the fields were ninety percent covered in solar panels. And while agrivoltaics weren't in and of themselves crow-proof, we'd equipped the solar panels with little spinning mirrors and evil eyes to keep the birds from getting too comfortable rooting around in the shade of the panels where the fruit would grow.

We did have plenty of panels, true, but that still left a thirty-yard open stretch to defend. Running the length of the fields, it amounted to around an acre — and some five thousand plants to protect. And that meant rocks. You see, birds hate to peck hard things. If you throw some red-painted rocks down before the fruit shows, they learn not to peck red things in the fields. More importantly, it fit the spirit of the farm, a place where we had left behind all the chemical warfare of the past — with its runoff, algal blooms, and carcinogens — and replaced it with purely psychological warfare.

Don't forget either that I really liked those crows — I grew them their own wild corn, after all. And while I winced at imagining pecking a rock myself — I knew well enough how poorly my teeth handled popcorn — anything was better than poisoning our friends. Even if, to my wife's dismay, it left our farm full of props…

There were rubber snakes to scare off squirrels, sheer curtains hanging over the few rows of wine grapes, and more than a few birdbaths in case thirst was their main motivation for attacking the berries. Add in my pack of guinea fowl for eating bugs, and you were left with my wife's *sometimes* affectionate name for the farm: The Bird Studio.

You may well wonder what my wife's alternative was. She was equally adamant about our shared beliefs of growing things naturally, of course, but she preferred to have soldiers on the ground. As if on cue, one of our seven cats approached, meowing as he rubbed against my leg.

"Hey, Bud," I said, making sure I didn't have paint on my hands before I stooped down to scratch his ears.

Bud was a true soldier, built like a tank the size of two cats and always ready for battle. He was dark brown, almost the same shade as the soil, which allowed him to army crawl around the farm year-round as he hunted for enemy combatants.

I didn't begrudge him his talents, of course. He certainly helped prevent rats — along with the urine of all his brothers and sisters-in-arms. I just didn't want him to be *too* successful. In the old days, they said housecats used to kill a billion birds each year, a horrifying statistic more suited to a genocide than a war where both sides scored some points. But I think we'd found a balance. We'd trained the cats to stay out of the forest, and by keeping the birds out of the fields, I could ensure the cats didn't have *too* many opportunities.

And that was the other crucial component of our farm's philosophy. After centuries of fighting Mother Nature — and nearly killing ourselves in the process — we and all the other farms in the area were finally following the 30% rule. As the theory went, humans could manage to live on a huge portion of the earth's surface, so long as we left 30% wild. That would act as a sink for biodiversity, ensuring we didn't threaten the fabric of nature that supported the life of everything we held dear.

For us, that meant the huge forest at the back of the property. It had started off smaller, but we added trees every year — sometimes with help from the corps — and by now it was a big, beautiful expanse, one that would only grow by the time our short lifespans on this land were finished.

"Cree-awwwww" a crow called from the tree line.

"Sorry, guys!" I called, turning to wave. "Enjoy the corn!"

I went back to the farmhouse with Bud on my heels. We might lose a few battles this year, but I would enjoy the fight, especially if the only thing getting hurt was a handful of strawberries.

The Restaurant

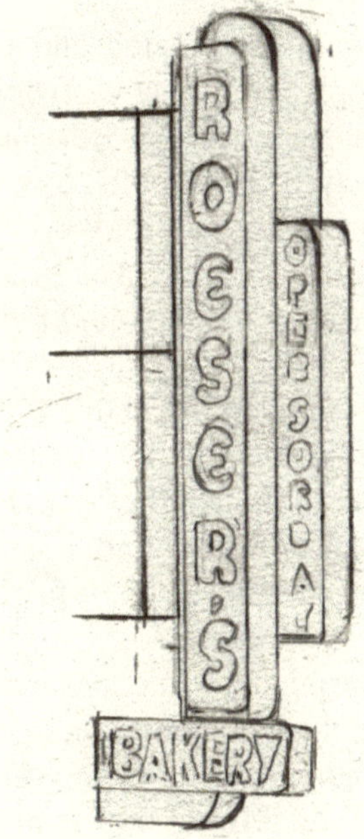

When did I start to savor life? Stubbornly, I refuse to believe it was only at the end. Even in the frantic days — the *beginning of the end,* if you will — I could at least see the irony in the way I was living, filling my schedule even as the world slid toward its doom. And I'd *tried* to explore my inner self, but I hadn't been *savoring,* not truly.

Not that there's any shame in just surviving. At first, I was pretty angry about the world falling apart, but in the end, my anger served no purpose. No matter what stage of life — single-celled organism, crawling, walking — life is always a mix of thinking deeply and getting by. It isn't easy. We're finite, embodied beings with only a hazy sense of the infinite. We fight, we cry, we love, we *make do*. But, sometimes, if we're really looking, we see the divine.

Still, even when I'm just scraping by now, I try to make time to savor my life. Here at the restaurant, we probably only get a dozen customers a night. They're government types, mostly — who else would be out and about? But given those numbers — and the general availability of post-apocalyptic produce — I only really have to make a single dish. And this, my friends, is how I have time to savor. That afternoon's shipment had a pound of buckwheat flour, two squashes, three heads of celery, a half-bottle of oil without identification (it smelled like canola), and a sprig of rosemary.

Maybe when I was younger, frenzied and frazzled, I would have thrown just such a meal together. I'm sure I would have loved it, too — no snob was I, even when there were grocery stores full of whatever I wanted. Still, I wouldn't have *exulted* in it. Now, though, the meal could be a symphony. I'd even call it yakisoba — because who alive could actually remember what real yakisoba tasted like? And my customers, with their ration cards for a single meal and a drab of whiskey, would probably love it too.

Even better than what I was cooking, though, was *when* I was cooking. Fall had finally come to Chicago. The restaurant was dark, the bartender not set to arrive for another hour, and the back door was open, ushering in a cool breeze from the lake. Never mind that the lake was two blocks further west than it had been in my youth, it felt amazing. Fall had been pushed back to November and December over the years, and the polar vertices that pounded us during the winter ensured it was short, but while we had it, I would savor that too. The hundred-year-old brick of the restaurant glowed in the fading sun, and everything was bliss.

I took the squash, carefully turning it over in my hands a few times. There were never bruises anymore, not with vertical farming being eighty percent of the supply, but the inspection was a critical first step. It showed the vegetable that you respected it, that you thought it capable of surprise. Then, I set it aside, letting it rest while I made the soba.

I sifted the flour — a mighty process unto itself, though it left a haze of dust floating through the kitchen that I stopped to admire, another preview of the brief winter to come. As I started to add water to the flour, I remembered my old cookbook, *Japanese Home Cooking*. I couldn't remember the chef's name — Sakai, maybe? — and hadn't seen the book in years, but it still stuck with me. She referred to making dough as a conversation, a constant back and forth between you and the soba, trying to get the feel right. I'm sure my dough was too clumpy, and I didn't have any tapioca to dust with, but man, was the conversation good. In the middle, it seemed like it might devolve into an argument, but eventually we got things right.

At last, the dough rolled out, I folded it over, slicing it into rough strips with my chef's knife. As I made a little mountain of noodles for my customers, I remembered the time I saw buckwheat in a field. It was in the '20s, obviously, before grid nationalization, when I'd still been a clean energy investor. I was touring some field in Washington, I think, with a farmer who wanted to lease it for solar.

He'd noticed me stopping to stare at the buckwheat. It had surprised me, I guess. More like knotweed than wheat, it had tall green stalks with tiny white flowers — like clovers grown way too tall — and they were waving in the wind like foam on some forgotten ocean. There had been a mountain in the background — hence my remembering it now — and the sun was burning bright.

"Used to grow a lot of that around here," the farmer had said, rubbing his hands together as he joined me. "Good cover crop, doesn't need much fertilizer. Of course, that was more than a hundred years ago. It's all corn now."

"Huh," I'd responded noncommittally, though what he said immediately buried itself in my brain. I have a mind for conversation, if not much else. Trauma brain, they used to call it, though I don't know how you'd refer to it now that we've been mass-traumatized. Still, it's sometimes easier for me to remember a conversation — and all the worry that goes into talking and people-pleasing — than it is for me to remember the actual events of my life.

After making the soba, I finally turned back to the squash. Washing and peeling, I made a neat pile of squash skin to bake later. Squash skin was murder in a recipe — texturally, that is — but I wouldn't be above eating a pile of squash chips in my time off. I suppose I could have composted it, but it was rare I wasted peels anymore. That was for truly inedible things, even though I'm sure my compost worms would have loved turning the little beige strips into soil.

I'd started getting into composting when I was thirty, well before the dark years. I'm glad I did, of course, but it had been a frantic, guilt-ridden thing — just like everything I did for the climate. Never mind that I was about forty years too late or that oil companies had covered up the issue until we were teetering on the brink of 1.5 degrees, I'd still wanted to do *something.*

More importantly, though, despite my handwringing and my moral scrupulosity — a particularly nasty form of OCD we'll talk more about later — composting was *fun.* Back then, I even had an electric composter, turning my scraps into soil in four hours even as it filled my house with funky air. You could buy more carbon filter pellets, but who would do that? (Late-stage capitalism demanded that you not even have the energy to click buy on things you thought you wanted).

I think I can admit I'm a much better gardener now. There were more than a few…*incidents* back then when I would invariably overwater, underwater, or anything in between. But with that composting soil, oh my stars, did things grow! I even grew carrots once on my porch. Unfortunately, my porch had been a shady, terrible place for growing vegetables. But even if the carrots never grew into more than knobby little things, their stalks were at least two feet tall. They'd certainly made a nice buffet for a couple of parsley worms. They polished off the whole patch in a single afternoon, but presumably they became swallowtail butterflies afterward, so at least I'd done something right…

—:—

An hour later, my squash finally roasting in the oven, the restaurant was a place transformed. Lucy, the bartender, had finally arrived, and we had lit every single candle, pouring what was hopefully an inviting light over the sidewalk. Lincoln Square had changed over the years — especially once the northwest side simply became the north side — but I liked to think I ran a cozy place. It was in one of the few original brick buildings left, which certainly gave me a head start, but hidden in the shade behind the Arizona refugee tower on Western, it felt like a well-kept secret.

Lucy was up front, slicing what little fruit we had behind the bar. There was a limit to how many drinks you could make without citrus, of course, but she was creative. Looking one last time in the oven at my tiny roasting babies, I joined her, grabbing a knife to help with the prep. We had grapes of all things. I hadn't seen a lemon in six months, but that wasn't unusual. Don't even get me started on how long it had been since I'd seen chocolate. I heard they had it on Mackinac again, but there was little chance of me traveling anytime soon.

"What'll these make?" I asked, grabbing a clump of grapes and a cutting board.

"I'm calling it whiskey jam," she said, tossing a handful of cut grapes into a bowl. "Half-muddled, half-garnished, gonna mix it with simple and cinnamon."

I raised an eyebrow, eyeing the pitifully empty cinnamon jar on the counter.

"A very small amount of cinnamon," she added, chuckling.

"Sounds pretty good," I said. "You should at least have enough for service tonight."

"Never more than a day," she quoted with a sly grin. She knew I hated the city's rebuilding song, but like everyone under thirty, she didn't see anything wrong with it. I mean, it *is* harmless, but something about the mayor commissioning an anodyne pop song to "boost our spirits" always grated at me. I suppose for all my talk about savoring life, I'm still a bit of a cynic. Or an Aquarius rising, or something like that… Still, I admired her optimism. She'd been just fifteen when things fell apart. She'd lost her father in the famines, too, but somehow, she managed to be a kind person — not to mention a terrific bartender.

"Yeah, yeah," I said, smiling as I rolled my eyes.

We worked in silence for a time, the scrape of the knives the only sound until the bell tinkled above the door.

A woman walked in, one I hadn't seen before, and unfortunately, she was gorgeous. She was small, probably five foot two or something, and she had that intangible blend of hardy and soft — something I hadn't realized I was attracted to before things fell apart — that had become just my type. Even worse, she was about my age, which meant I couldn't dismiss my attraction out of hand.

Not that there's anything wrong with being drop dead gorgeous, of course. It's just that pretty women tend to trigger my OCD and the crushing guilt so central to my personality. First off, I feel guilty for thinking they're attractive in the first place. After all, what if that means I'm objectifying them? I'm a feminist, so I mean no disrespect, but it's not like I'm viewing their beauty objectively like I would a waterfall or a tree or something.

You could argue that desire is natural, I guess — so long as it's framed by things like compassion, consent, and mutually recognized humanity — but I just couldn't get my brain to see it that way. Beyond that, though, it felt laughable to even consider such a thing. I'd lost enough, had *ruined* enough in my life, that I knew it would be best to die alone. So why even bother feeling the flutter in my chest? It wouldn't do any good, just another reason to crumple up my heart like a paper bag.

Luckily, I have Pure O — purely obsessional OCD — so I don't have to perform any sort of visible tick, but I do have to *imagine* myself doing the exact opposite of what I'm afraid of. In this case, I'd always figured the opposite of attraction was respect, so I pictured myself giving her a firm handshake. Then, like any self-respecting business owner, I suppressed the urge to gulp, forcing a smile to my face as I came around the counter.

"Welcome," I said, hooking my thumbs on my apron in what I hoped was an inoffensive way. "First time?"

"Yes," she said, smiling in return, which only made her more damningly fetching. "It's just me, though. I hope that's alright?"

"Of course," I said, pointing in the direction of my best table. It was by the windows but near enough to the fireplace to feel both open and cozy. "You're never alone when you're here."

"You might have to copyright that," she said with a grin.

She took off her jacket, revealing an ensemble that was also unfortunately just my type: hiking boots with tall wool socks, canvas pants, and a shirt with front pockets where she actually stored a notebook. It was almost too majestic to take in and still remember how to breathe. I joined her at her table with a pitcher of water — something my city, at least, still had in ample supply — where I filled her glass.

"We have yakisoba tonight," I said. "And if you're drinking, our mixologist is making her signature whiskey jam."

The woman's eyes drifted to the bar, where Lucy waved.

"That sounds lovely," she said, her eyes glittering in the candlelight as she looked back at me. Her gaze had a weight to it, the kind of person who was actually present with others — a rare gift at any time in human history, but especially so after the hell we'd all been through.

"I heard about this place from some colleagues," she added. "They had to head back early, but they said you're the real deal, an actual local and everything."

"I guess I know the area," I said, laughing. "I've lived here since the twenties, but I'm not famous or anything."

She nodded, likely considering her own ancient history.

"Well," she said, "I think it's lovely. Maybe you can give me some directions after dinner. You take project credits, right?"

"That's most of our business," I said, nodding. "You can just show me your badge before you leave. Are you in for the big build?"

We live, of course, in a time of renewed hope. During the dark years, despite an emergency not being announced until millions were dead, we did *sort of* rally as a people. We started capturing carbon en masse, something that had cost \$600/ton in my old corporate days. We did enough to stop the bleeding, I suppose, but it takes a long time to get all that poison out of the air, even when it's a federal enterprise. So, in the meantime, there's still plenty of projects to do, like doubling the size of the flood tunnels under the streets of Chicago — a network that had been hundreds of miles long even before the worst. At any rate, the build had brought thousands of builders and engineers to the area, something my little restaurant desperately needed.

"I am," she said. "I'm an ecologist, though, so I'm just here to bother them while they dig."

"Damn," I said by accident, just barely holding back the 'that's sexy' on the other end of my sentence.

"Not a fan of green space?" she asked.

"No, no," I said quickly. "I'm just impressed. We're usually stuck with stuffy engineers."

At that moment, the door opened again, revealing a regular, Sean, who was just such a stuffy structural engineer.

"I'll get your plate started," I said to the woman, waving at Sean as I pointed to his regular table. "Lucy will be over with a drink. Just holler if you need anything else, and I'll stop by when you're done for those directions."

I scurried toward the kitchen, my palms sweating. And here I'd thought it would be a normal night…

—:—

Service flew by, the night blessedly busy enough to keep my mind off the beautiful woman out front. Well, not entirely… Even Lucy, punk kid that she was, stuck her head into the kitchen to harass me.

"I saw you with that woman," she said. "Let me know if you need me to drop off a love letter or anything."

I think I threw a towel at her head, though I can't really remember, elbow-deep in noodles as I was. Still, everyone got fed, and we sold fifteen plates, which was pretty damn good for us back then. Lucy, as always, did a little better on drinks, averaging one and a half per person.

When everyone had finished — and we'd dropped off what was left of the grapes for dessert — I came back out front to help cash out. The woman still sat at her table, looking out the window as she slowly sipped her second drink. As I'd said, the bills were mostly paid in project credits, and Lucy read out the long badge numbers as I frantically tapped them into my phone. Still, most of the regulars were good tippers, and by the end of the night, I was at least sure we'd have enough to stay open one more day.

Finally, apron-less and clad in the cozy fall jacket I only got to use once or twice a year, I approached the woman's table. We'd already cashed her out, and I'd gotten her name — Elena — but as I introduced myself, she told me she preferred Ellie.

"So," I said, "I'm happy to give you directions, but I probably won't be any better than an app."

Not that apps were monolithic like they used to be… Along with the telecom collapse, there just weren't as many *things* as there used to be. I don't know where it falls in Maslow's hierarchy, but 'business services' proved to be more of a nice-to-have. When people spent most of their time trying to stay alive, there just wasn't time to do much else, let alone do something like review a restaurant.

"Well," Ellie said, "that's kind of my problem. It seems this place isn't on any of the apps. It might not even be open, but I figured since you knew the neighborhood…"

"Sure. I don't have anything going on if you want to walk around a bit."

"That'd be great," she said, flashing her million-watt smile again as she stood. Suffice it to say I was smitten, but it's not nothing when someone touches your heart through a hundred layers of scar tissue. I used to think my capacity for suffering was infinite, heading into the breach again and again for the sake of — if not *love,* exactly, perhaps hope — but every misstep seemed to break me just a little more. By the time Ellie walked into the restaurant, it really had seemed strange to even find a woman charming again.

We went out onto the landing — my restaurant being on the second floor — and snaked our way down the metal steps. The night was cool, and I found myself looking up at the sky, watching as my breath floated away as fog.

"So," I said, stopping at the bottom, the square still bustling with people, "what are we looking for?"

"A record store," Ellie said, looking around as if she might have missed it on her way in. "I've only seen it in a picture, but it was called Victory Vinyl."

"Oh, yeah," I said, frowning as I tried to picture it. "Yellow sign, kind of messy?"

She nodded. "You know it?"

"Sort of. The owner was kind of a dick, but I'm pretty sure it was up on Argyle — assuming it's still open. The guy who owned it was ancient, but I'm happy to walk up there."

"Alright," she said, smiling — the gesture apparently instinctual with her in spite of everything. "Thank you."

We started walking north, under the new mural, the giant German men with tubas laughing as they towered over us. The old mural — the one of a peaceful German village overlooking a river — had been destroyed in the flooding, ironically enough. And now… Well, there probably weren't enough Germans left in the neighborhood to start a basketball team, but the tradition was nice, at least. Besides, we had to keep something. Like my restaurant, there was precious little left of the old brick two-flats that had filled the neighborhood in the before. The sheer speed of rebuilding in the city had ensured everything was metal and concrete, but it was better than sleeping on the streets.

"Have you been to Chicago before?" I asked as we walked up Lincoln.

"It's been a loooong time," she said, looking around at the buildings. "I'm based out of Little Rock normally since I work with hyperaccumulators — lithium agromining and all that."

My heart skipped a beat, my face going blank. Luckily, I knew what she was talking about, but her casual-cool-genius vibe only added to her appeal — not to mention reminding me of a doomed relationship from twenty years earlier I thought I'd forgotten.

"Sorry," she added, blushing, "talking shop again."

"No, no," I said, forcing myself to smile as I put up a hand. "I'm familiar, I'm just…impressed again, I guess. I hadn't thought you could get any cooler."

"Stop," she said, pushing me on the shoulder.

The motion felt oddly familiar, but we were quiet for a moment afterward, her eyes moving back to the sidewalk as if she thought she'd overstepped. The other woman, by the way — the one from my memories — had been a biomedical engineer. I like women that are too smart for me, I guess… I'd been in my thirties when that particular tragedy played out, but I tried to push it from my mind. This new woman may have completely discombobulated me, but I still knew instinctually that it was bad practice to dwell on the ghost of another woman when you had a live one right in front of you.

"So, why Chicago then?" I asked. "Pretty sure there's no lithium up here."

She sighed, nodding.

"Well, mostly the weather," she joked before turning serious. "I have some family up here, but we lost touch. I thought… Well, I *hoped* if I took this assignment I could find them — my sister, at least."

The words seemed to have cost her a lot, so I just nodded.

We reached Lawrence, walking into the night market. Thankfully, ever since the city rebuilt, around sixty percent of the streets stayed closed to cars — not that many people used them anymore anyway. You still had to make sure you didn't get clipped in the bike lane, but otherwise, Western and Lawrence was buzzing, teeming with vendors selling all kinds of odds and ends. A lot of it was reclaimed — repaired clothing, driftwood art, even one dubious-looking booth with gold watches — presumably scavenged from the flooded condos beyond the water line.

Ellie, at least, seemed delighted, stopping at most of the booths and chatting with the vendors. The first time, she looked at me apologetically, but I smiled — where did I have to be? — so she carried on. The vendors seemed equally delighted, her magnetism apparently universal. That was a double-edged sword, of course. It meant I was right about her, confirming she was something special. But as with all charming extroverts, I had to admit she may simply be like the sun. She warmed my husk of a dying planet, sure, but she beamed her light without discrimination.

We eventually made our way through the market, following Lincoln as it bent toward the northwest. As soon as we approached Argyle, though, it was clear we weren't going to find what we were looking for. The entire corner was dark, the invisible hand of government rebuilding apparently not this far west yet. It looked like they had dealt with flooding at one time, the door still barricaded with sandbags and the edges of the sidewalk caked with mud.

"This is the place," I said, "or what's left of it."

We stepped up to the grimy windows, peering into the darkness of the store. There were boxes everywhere, some of the shelves still intact and filled with records. Ironically, it reminded me of the legendary Southside record store, Dusty Groove. Somehow, though, I don't think even they could sell records *this* dusty.

"Your sister worked here?" I asked, pulling back from the glass I was fogging with my breath. She stayed where she was, her hands cupped on the sides of her face, but she nodded.

"I lost her number," she said. "Or everyone did. It was the telecom collapse. She'd just moved up here, trying to get a break from the family, I guess. But I hadn't thought it would be a twenty-year break. By the time things settled… Well, I haven't been able to find her online, that's for sure."

"That's hard," I said, wanting to pat her on the shoulder or something but not feeling able to.

"No harder than anyone else," she said, finally turning away from the store.

Despite the dim on the street, a flash of yellow caught my eye. I moved along the window, finding a bright piece of paper taped to the inside.

We've closed, it said, *but it's not over. If you want records, come to—*

There was an address without a phone number, but it looked like it might be on the Brown Line.

"Maybe it's not hopeless," I said, pointing at the poster.

She hurried over, pulling out a notebook as she wrote down the address. She looked at the street behind her, perhaps hoping the secret of the address would reveal itself like a waypoint in a video game. Chicago was still on a grid, thankfully, but the address was at least five miles away.

"Look," I said, "I'm off tomorrow. I'm happy to find this place with you — as long as you're game to do a little grocery shopping on the way back."

She met my eyes, searching for them for something. But finally, she smiled again.

"Alright," she said. "I'd like that."

—:—

I woke up early the next morning, the sun just starting to rise. I've always been an early riser, though I usually lay in bed for an hour with a book. For some reason, though, that day, I pushed myself out of bed, wandering to the window where I found what could only be described as a perfect fall sky. Even as a patch of soft clouds settled over the colorful trees, an edge of sun broke through. Not enough to light the streets, but for a moment, a few golden rays cut across the city, hitting only the tallest tree, its leaves shining like a beacon.

Oddly enough, ever since things fell apart, I couldn't look at something beautiful without thinking of some kind of suffering. Somewhere in the world, for example, a hurricane was probably bearing down on the few people who remained on the world's coasts. It didn't detract from the beauty — this *simultaneity* — but it did act as a reminder again to savor what we still had left. Even as we had to — as human beings, if nothing else — take responsibility for each other's suffering and fight for a better world, we also had to look toward the light.

Ellie would be meeting me by the train, but I still had a couple hours. Given my penchant to fill every spare moment with some sort of frenetic activity, I decided to make pancakes. It's always better to celebrate your day off with something special you wouldn't normally cook, but I also can't stand meditating for more than a few minutes, and it wouldn't have been worth the energy credit to shower, either.

I wandered toward the kitchen, the long hallway of my Chicago apartment like a cave. On the other end, the kitchen faced east, and the mottled light from before danced along the tile floor, shining onto all the little knickknacks I'd managed to collect in the decade since I'd moved in. I checked my battery by the back door, the little wind rotor on my porch apparently keeping it sufficiently full during the night. Flipping a breaker, I diverted some of the power to my griddle so it could heat.

Now, the real challenge with making pancakes — or anything these days — is the moment when your aspirations meet the reality of food scarcity. As I'm sure you realized with the yakisoba, perfect results aren't always possible. But with something like pancakes, there are certain…structural elements that can't be done without. You need some kind of starch, which needs to be bound by some kind of protein, and ideally, something that will give it all a rise. There's more than one way to accomplish each of those, of course, but it isn't like a salad where you can just throw it all together and call it done.

My fridge was rather sad. Seeing as how I was at the restaurant all the time, I didn't have anywhere near the gardening capacity of some of my neighbors — though I did enough pitching in to get by on everyone else's kindness. To that end, I did have a half-dozen eggs for helping my neighbor Micky rebuild his henhouse. I didn't have any milk, but I did have an old tub of yogurt, which worked weirdly well when mixed with water.

Nodding to myself, I moved to the little pantry cupboard. This, in contrast, was filled with odds and ends I couldn't cook at the restaurant. Opening it to the morning light, it looked like a treasure chest, the assorted glass bottles glittering in their many shapes and colors. I stopped to stare at them, reminding myself to say a prayer of thanks again for the plastic ban they'd finally implemented in the late thirties.

I picked up my tall green flour jar, holding it up to the light. It looked more like a bottle of sand art, swirling with a mess of colors. I'd taken to dragging home whatever spare flour I couldn't get through at the restaurant, which meant my personal stash was a chimera of wheat, rye, potato, and spelt. I shrugged, putting it on the counter while I hunted for the baking soda. That's the beauty of eternal solitude, I suppose. Only when you're accountable for another person's happiness does the quality of your pancakes begin to truly matter.

Looking at it another way, though, for whatever reason, there's always been this sort of fundamental laziness about me. Or maybe I should call it exhaustion. It didn't set in until I was an adult, but it never really left, and there's some things I just never have the heart to do well. There's plenty of things I take pride in, of course — including the restaurant — but once I'm cooking for myself, I have to really work at the whole savoring thing. Just like the socks I still darn, I've never gotten better at it, just limping along, my feet in some sort of woolen Ship of Theseus that hardly sails.

At any rate, as I mixed the ingredients together, I tried to remind myself to be grateful. *You lived. You're still alive. You get to eat, and pancakes, no less. Savor this moment, embrace the infinite oneness of...pancakes.* Even I had to laugh at that last part, but in a way, it did work. My whisking became more...*enlightened* somehow. Maybe it's just the mental illness — my brain so full of anxious thoughts there's nothing left over — but this was the morning, dammit! Shouldn't my tank be full?

As I put a slice of butter in the griddle, I thought of my ancestors. Something about butter always harkened back to olden times for me, even if I wasn't churning it myself. On that morning, though, it felt more like a condemnation. *This is what became of our genes?* my ancestors seemed to say. How had they borne the drudgery? Surely part of it was chauvinism, dropping most of the work on their wives. Still, there was something I was missing, some secret to how they worked each day, sure the sun would rise again.

As I held the bowl over the griddle, prepared to dump all of my batter into a single mega pancake — so as to make my cooking process *even* lazier — I stopped. My ancestors would have made individual pancakes, and they would have made about a hundred to feed — in my grandfather's case — a fourteen-person family. So I reached into the silverware drawer and took out a ladle. And as I formed each pancake — perhaps not lovingly, but certainly mindfully — I felt what seemed to be a glimmer of peace.

—:—

As the train rolled down the track, Ellie was taking full advantage of the window seat, her face pressed up against the glass like a kid at the zoo. While she looked undeniably adorable, I wasn't far behind, craning my neck to see too. It was a rare pleasure these days to be on one of the old El lines, rumbling past the buildings like some kind of metal beast in an elaborately carved cavern.

The new lines — the ring lines that arced toward the west — had been tunneled, allowing them to go right beneath existing neighborhoods. That was all well and good technologically since America seemed to have completely forgotten how to make sacrifices for infrastructure, but that also meant they were underground. Long and cave-like, the silver and bronze lines didn't really live up to their names, delegating us to the dismal darkness of every other city's transit.

After a few stops, we came to Montrose, the brown line curving to the south like a hungry snake. I craned my neck to look for Margie's, the once candy shop — or its building, anyway — thankfully still standing proudly just past the station's steps. They'd always had a classic Fifties feel, selling pies and handmade candy alongside shakes and banana splits. Even in the internet age — or perhaps *because* of the internet age — I had always found refuge there, either taking a long walk to get there or sitting inside while I drowned my sorrows in sugar.

One time, I had gone in on Halloween night, jamming into a corner with a slice of pumpkin pie and two mountains of whipped cream. Kids pressed against the glass in costume, apparently lured in by the candy even as their pillowcases burst with the kind of manufactured sweetness you couldn't find anymore. One kid actually tugged on their parent's sleeve and pointed at me, asking why 'that old man is alone.' I'd held up my pumpkin pie as if that would explain my solitude.

"Did I miss something good?" Ellie asked, trying to look back as the train sped onward.

"Just an old ice cream shop," I said.

Her eyes widened, taking on a faraway look.

"Do you remember all the fucking ice cream?" she asked, sighing. "I mean the real stuff, when you could have it any time you wanted."

"In any flavor," I added.

"Was it a good shop?" she asked. "Wait, don't tell me. Or do. I can't decide."

Instead of telling her about the pumpkin pie, I told her about the time my brother and I had gone there on a Sunday night. It had been in the summer, so the line was out the door, and they were rapidly running out of everything. When our turn finally came, my brother had asked for mint chocolate chip — mention of this flavor alone earning a jealous frown from Ellie — but they'd run out. Chocolate? Out. Strawberry? Out. After six or seven flavors, my brother had looked the ice cream man dead in the eye and asked if he was on TV, sure he was being punked.

From there — like it always seemed to with Ellie — the conversation took on a mind of its own. We talked about everything, including life before, which was rare enough those days. And oddly enough, even knowing it wasn't a date, even knowing — as I've just told you — how utterly unqualified I was to love another person, I felt the buzz of that familiar electricity.

It's a heady time, when the outlines of someone are taking shape, and you think they might just be the thing your soul's been searching for. But something was different, too. Perhaps finally taking my own advice, I knew I should savor my time with this impeccable woman. We would find her sister, she would leave, and that would be that. And so I really listened. I really looked.

Still, it was hard not to see in her all the other mistakes I'd made, all the other women I'd loved and lost. Relationship OCD — another mask on my many-faced demon — comes from just such a pile of regrets. For me, it's an extension of my moral scrupulosity, an obsession that I'll fail and hurt someone else, that I'll have one more regret, a regret that proves to be one too many, finally cracking my mind into a thousand pieces.

I, by the way, am an absolute delight to break up with. I always understand, always see why you reached your conclusion. I wish you well on your future voyages and remain friends with at least sixty percent of my exes — when it was still possible to stay in touch with people, anyway. Now, though, any time I've considered love, I spend more time thinking about the fall than the view. It may sound like a fear of commitment, but it's not. It's a fear of doing wrong, of hurting someone again. Part of me seems to think if I obsess enough about our fit, then we both might avoid disaster.

Ellie finally turned, putting her back to the train window, the conversation somehow having a bigger appeal to her than the view.

"So," she said, "you love it here, huh?"

"I do," I said honestly. "It's funny to say that. I guess people don't really get choices anymore, but I suppose I'd be here even if everything hadn't gone… Well, you know. What about you? Is there any place you'd choose if you could?"

"Maybe," she said, getting a faraway look. "I think after everything — not just the planet, but my family, my sister — I just wanted to choose…*nothing*. Moving around's been nice. Being on these projects, I think I'm more hopeful than the average person these days. It's just… Well, the future of nothing is nothing, you know?"

"I wouldn't be so sure," I said. "Choosing can be just as dangerous. You think you know what's gonna happen, and then you choke out any surprise life has left for you. I…" I stopped, looking at the floor. "I guess I don't know what I'm saying, but if you do wanna stay a while, Chicago would be lucky to have you."

"Thanks," she said, touching my arm. Even through my jacket, it felt electric. *Don't kid yourself,* I thought, trying to get a handle on the little match of hope flickering feebly in my heart.

Just then, the recording clicked on, the dulcet tones of Lee Crooks announcing our destination. I have a pet theory that if we ever abandon those recordings from 1998, the city will really descend into rioting. Even if the end of the world hadn't done it — at least not as much as you'd think — *that* would. But there wasn't time to consider all of this, let alone share it with Ellie. Fifteen seconds isn't all that long, and before the doors could close again, we were off the train and on our way.

She smiled at me as we crossed the platform, and I smiled back, desperate not to waste this perfect day on worry. Besides, what could go wrong? I'd already given up on love, and after a wonderful afternoon, I'd let this beautiful woman walk back out of my life. What justification could I possibly have for subjecting another woman to my brokenness? At least that way no one would get hurt. At least I could rest knowing the damage I'd done was in the past.

—:—

By the time we'd made our stop and got back on the train, it was already late afternoon, the feeble autumn sun already keen on giving up, relinquishing its power to the night. We'd found the man who owned the record store, the address leading us to an old row house. He even remembered Ellie's sister, giving her the last phone number he had for her. When we got back to the street, politely declining the man's invitation to tea, Ellie had stared at the scrap of paper for a long time, like a diver who'd finally returned to the surface with a pearl only to forget what it was for.

"Do you…want to call her?" I asked, reaching into my pocket in case she needed my phone.

"Not yet," she said, shaking her head as she looked up. "I need to collect myself, I think. But let's go to that market. You spent all this time helping me; it's about time we did something for you."

"Alright," I said slowly. "If you're sure."

"I am, really," she said, stuffing the paper into her pocket. "Let's go."

Still, despite her initial cheerfulness, by the time we made it back to the train, she looked lost again. Her stare was just as intent as before, only now it fell haphazardly, her gaze straying toward whatever was closest: a train seat, a pamphlet, a concrete wall.

As we reached the market, though, I was glad I'd dragged her along. It was massive and chaotic, and it was by far my favorite place in the city. And she seemed to love it too, the sparkle crawling back into her eyes as she tried to take in all the stalls. They'd built it over Welles Park, a sprawling glass enclosure that sat on top of a newly designed geothermal field, keeping the place comfortable all year round.

To me, it was a hopeful place, a place where being a human felt like it might be a good thing after all. *See?* it seemed to say. *We can have an economy without trying to extinct ourselves. Did we rebase the dollar? Sure! Do we run everything like a giant private-public partnership? Of course! But what kind of guns and butter bullshit was GDP measuring anyway? Who cares if we produce another thousand widgets when the planet is dying?*

This was better, anyway. Don't get me wrong, we still desperately need the staple crops they were churning out from the indoor farms. But while they got farmland up and running again, it had inadvertently turned everything else into a charming farmer's market. One man was selling squash that he'd probably grown on his roof, each one a different shape. You could probably write a whole new branch of psychology on which misshapen gourd appealed to your sensibilities — or at least an online quiz. But it was all like that: magical, whimsical, filled with delight.

But best of all, Ellie seemed to sense this magic, the bottomless potential of the quotidian. And unlike me, who just floated through the market anonymously until I found the sellers I knew, she talked to every person who met her eyes — even if it was only a word or two.

"Tell me about these marvelous carrots," she'd say as the vendor's eyes lit up. And even when my guesses were right — they grew them in an old tire by the river — learning the truth was even better than my imagination.

As we turned into the next row, my usual vendor waving as she saw me, Ellie noticed someone with cookies.

"Oh my God, my sister loved these," she said. She grabbed my hand, dragging me toward them. Suddenly, though, I seemed to be floating, my brain no longer connected to my feet. Her hand was warm despite the chilly air, not like a furnace but like a sun, immediately the center of my useless little universe. She didn't seem to notice — the gesture much more about instantly redirecting me toward the cookies — but for me, it was like shock therapy, a thousand little explosions setting off in my heart.

"Wow," she breathed, leaning over the cookies, her hands fluttering as if they wanted to touch them. They looked like deep dish pizzas, some kind of tin cookie with layers of caramel and nuts. Their mere size seemed like a resounding endorsement of humanity's progress, not to mention our ability to actually indulge in something again.

"My sister loved these," she said again to no one in particular, her eyes suddenly sad.

"We've been baking them in the same store for thirty years," the baker said, smiling, "give or take a few of the bad ones…" She was about my age, and Ellie nodded along as she spoke, as if searching the woman's eyes for signs of her sister.

"How long do they last?" she asked, no doubt calculating if she could buy one now and keep it until her sister turned up.

"I'll just be over there," I said gently, touching her shoulder as I nodded my head toward my vendor. She deserved to do this on her own, the cookie-buying suddenly transformed into a sacred ritual — and the cookie woman the only qualified priestess. She nodded absently, though she still flashed me one of the most beautiful smiles I'd ever seen.

I walked toward Nada, my vendor, a sly smile coming to her face. I'd been coming to her for years, since before she took over from her mom. Somehow, she still gave off the same just-smoked-a-blunt attitude, her chillness at once utterly delightful and completely out of step with running a business. She told me once when she was younger that she used to hide from her mom for entire days during the harvest to avoid work, and she still seemed to be hiding, even as the produce kept somehow appearing at the market.

"Heyyyy," she said, drawing out the word as I walked up. "Who's that you're with?"

"Just a friend," I said, my voice rather unconvincing.

"Sure," she said, "and this is just produce."

"It is just produce, though, right?" I asked, cocking an eyebrow as I looked at her table.

"Suuuuure," she said, smiling.

There was a huge pile of squash, presumably deep enough to hide drugs or whatever else she was hinting at, but my attention was immediately grabbed by a bushel of apples in the center. Ever since the apple crop was decimated by the change in weather — later frosts, unpredictable rains — I hardly ever saw them anymore. I knew they were working on indoor varietals, but new apples took at least a decade to perfect, and even longer for consistency. In fact, where I'd held intense apple opinions in the old days, I couldn't even tell you what kind these were. They were a sort of mottled pink and red, like a basket of maple leaves.

"Where did you get these?" I asked, taking one in my hand. Normally it was bad form to touch the produce at the market, but Nada knew me well enough — and probably wouldn't have cared besides. But she gave me a nod and I took a bite, a thousand memories seeming to fire along my synapses at once.

"You won't believe me," she said, "but they're from out back."

I had seen her farm once. It was about an hour outside the city, and it was sort of in reverse, the farmhouse back against a river while the fields stretched toward the road. The fields were dotted with LED grow sheds now, but they still grew what they could outside when the seasons allowed. There had been trees along the river, but I didn't remember any fruit trees.

"Out back…" I said, staring into the juicy bite I'd left in the apple.

"The ones by the river," she said. I remembered trees, but those had been huge… I had taken them for oaks.

"They stopped fruiting years ago," she said, "but they kept getting taller, way taller than orchard trees should be. And this year, they just started growing fruit again."

"Wow," I said, taking another bite. Maybe we weren't doomed after all. I needed flour, and I needed a dozen other things for the restaurant — more than my credits would buy — but I suddenly tried to remember how much my bank account had in it, how much I could risk to bring these apples to every single person I could.

"How many will you sell me?"

—:—

It wasn't until noon the next day, when Lucy finally got to the restaurant, that I realized how deep a hole I had dug for myself.

"What are you *doing?*" she asked, dropping her bag in the doorway to the kitchen, her eyes wide.

I was elbow-deep in apples, a giant clear tub from my apartment building's basement the only thing capable of holding the sheer volume I had bought. In the end, Nada had shut down her stall, driving me to the restaurant with a bushel and a half — and emptying my bank account in the process. She'd thrown in some flour and a ten-year-old tin of cinnamon she'd found on the farm, but the pressure was on.

"I'm peeling apples," I said without stopping to look up. I already had a pile of pink skins about a half-foot high, and I'd have to move fast to turn them into a half-dozen other things before they browned too much. Apple chips, syrup, vinegar, all of it in a manic attempt to preserve every ounce of fall's essence before it slipped away, before I went another decade without these lightning bolt memories on my tongue.

"But…why?" she asked. "And why so many?"

"Because!" I said, shaking an apple in the air. "Our customers will remember this, they *need* this. It's proof that things grow, that there's, you know, hope and stuff. It's— Is this a terrible idea?"

"I don't know," she said, laughing as she picked up her things, hanging them on the coat rack. "I barely remember apples."

"Have one!" I said, gesturing to the tub. "They're perfect."

She stepped up to the tub, looking down into the ocean of pink. Each apple was like its own little world floating in space, even the restaurant's rebuild LED lights no match for their charming color.

I nodded, urging her to take one. She picked one off the top, holding it by just two fingers. She turned it over, looking at it from top to bottom.

"How do you eat it?" she asked.

"Just…eat it," I said. I picked one up, making a show of taking a big bite.

She pointed at the pile of shavings.

"You eat the skin?" she asked.

"If you want," I said. "I'm just peeling these ones for pie."

She took her own bite, albeit smaller than mine, staring up at the ceiling while she chewed slowly.

"It's nothing special," she finally said, setting the rest down on the stainless-steel table.

"Nothing special?" I asked, finally stopping with my hands still in the tub. "Don't you taste the *hope?* The…the possibility?"

"No," she said, chuckling as she went over to the spice racks to do her own prep.

My shoulders slumped after that, but I refused to give up, pushing onward through the mountain before me. I guess the young would have their own delicacies, their own nostalgia built up around what was essentially the randomness of harvest. It was actually laughable that our generation had thought we could have 'classics,' as if we could really go on eating the same things our grandparents had as we destroyed the earth. Still, my customers would remember. And when I had new customers — *younger* customers — I would find out what their favorite dish was, the food that would make them stop and stare at their plate in disbelief.

Crossing the kitchen again with a basket of spices, Lucy stopped, dropping them in front of me.

"Do these work with apple, you think?" she asked, taking out the nutmeg and looking at it doubtfully.

"They're perfect," I said, sighing. "Just follow your nose. You have a gift, remember?"

She shrugged, picking up the box to head into the dining room. But as she reached the door, she stopped, looking back.

"Are you in love or something?" she asked, a sly look in her eyes.

"You've been hanging out with that woman from Saturday dinner, haven't you?"

"*That*," I said, shaking an apple at her, "has nothing to do with this."

"Sure, sure," she said, heading to the bar. "Whatever you have to tell yourself."

"Not that you have anything to worry about!" I called after her.

She waved over her shoulder, content to ignore me as she set up the bar. Lucy's mother had remarried during the rebuilding, and I could tell it had hurt her — not to mention her stepdad being a bit of a prick. Not that I thought highly enough of myself to assume I was a father figure to her… But we split the profits from the restaurant — nonexistent though they were — and I didn't want her thinking I would jeopardize her attempts to save up and get her own place. Even if I seemed senile for daring to dream, it wasn't as if a beautiful woman like Ellie was about to ask me to leave Chicago with her.

The clock chimed, and I got back to work, my own self-imposed problems with the apples bearing down on me like a freight train.

—:—

In the end, we managed to make two dozen pies. I blew through the restaurant's solar battery running the oven — almost certainly forcing us to close the next day — but standing in the kitchen in front of all those steaming pies, I couldn't help but feel it was worth it. The rest of the meal was more or less an afterthought — a bunch of kale borrowed from our neighbors turned into a fall salad with heaping bowls of apple skin chips — but the pies were a masterpiece, quite possibly my life's work.

I dished up another tray, ready to rush them to the dining room. The first few guests had already come and gone, almost all of them buying an extra pie to go as I shot smug looks over my shoulder at Lucy. I earned a few healthy eye rolls for my trouble, but she had risen to the occasion, too. She ended up doing fall hot toddies, earning just as many accolades for the apple syrup she'd blended with the whiskey and tea.

As I was heading back to the kitchen, the doorbell rang, a man I didn't know sticking his head in the door as a half-dozen others waited behind him on the landing.

"Hey," he said, looking around. "You the one with the pies?"

"I am," I said, beckoning them inside. "Sit anywhere you like."

The man pointed at the far corner, and I pulled together a couple of tables to fit all his friends. I'd never seen any of them before, actually, the word possibly spreading farther than I'd intended. But as I explained the menu, pointing to Lucy for the drinks, one of them, a youngish woman, nodded knowingly.

"I've heard about the drinks here," she said, smiling sheepishly. The man who'd stuck his head in gave her an odd look — her father, perhaps? — but he ordered drinks for the table anyway.

"Do you guys live on the square?" I asked. "It's rare to have our reputation precede us. Normally people just wander in here on a whim."

"We're in the Arizona," another man in the group said. "But it's the first time I've seen pie being sold since I got here."

"Yeah," the first man agreed, "thought there'd be way more fruit when we moved north, but I guess it's the same everywhere."

I explained — as briefly as I could, given my out-of-control enthusiasm — about Nada's trees, about things growing where I hadn't thought they would. And to their credit, they listened to me, enraptured until Lucy tapped me on the elbow to make room for their drinks.

"And that," I said, raising a finger, "is my signal to go get the pie."

I'd like to think it was my stirring speech, but the Arizonans loved the pie. And after they left, they spread the word even more, sending at least a dozen of their friends over: children, spouses, and grandparents in tow as they all came to try the "famous" pie. I had little time for speeches after that — the tables filling faster than I could clean them — but we sold through everything on the menu, not even the whiskey holding out as closing time approached.

I was ringing up my last table, a couple of out-of-town regulars who seemed baffled by the crowds, when the door chimed. I looked up to find Ellie, standing in her raincoat, her hair wet and her makeup running. When had it even started to rain? I thanked the customers before dashing over, taking her by the elbow on instinct. But as I guided her to a table, signaling for Lucy to bring some tea, I noticed there was more than rain coming down her cheeks.

"Are you alright?" I asked, easing her into a chair as if she might break.

"I'm fine," she said, sniffling as she forced herself to smile, taking a mug from Lucy who'd dashed over.

"It's my sister," she said, taking a deep breath. "I just needed to talk to someone, and I didn't know where else to go."

"I'm glad you came," I said. I looked toward the kitchen, nodding for Lucy to leave, to let me handle the dishes and the register. I sat, taking Ellie's hand, her fingers like ice.

"Tell me what happened."

—:—

"My sister is dead," Ellie said, her voice choking as she had to say that awful final word.

As if just realizing I had taken her hand, I let it go, blinking in stunned silence.

"Ellie, I'm so sorry," I managed to say, forcing a hand to her shoulder so I wasn't leaving her completely abandoned in her grief.

I'm still not sure why the news hurt me so badly. I had only known this woman a few days — and had never met her sister, of course — but somehow, looking for her sister had made the woman real. And after everything I'd seen, all the countless dead sacrificed to our greed, it still felt wrong when someone died now. We were meant to be on the other side, our sins already paid for.

"What happened?"

"Cancer," she said, laughing desperately even as more tears came. "Who the fuck dies of cancer anymore?"

"Yeah," I said, shaking my head. "How did you find out?"

"It was anticlimactic, really," she said, staring into the table. "As soon as I got back to my hotel, I called the number and asked for her. It ended up being her girlfriend — someone I never knew, obviously — but..."

She shut her eyes, squeezing out a tear as her voice caught.

"I was ten years late. She survived everything else, but she got cancer, and they couldn't treat it with everything so broken."

She let out a single sob before she wiped her cheeks, looking at me again.

"I just wish she had called. If only I had known, if..."

"You're alright," I said, taking her hand. "Things were different then — for all of us. But you looked for her now, and I'm sure she appreciates it, wherever she is."

"Yeah," she said quietly, nodding sadly. "Thank you."

I sighed, nodding.

"I can't do much, but I do have pie."

She laughed again, reaching for a hanky to blow her nose.

"I'd love some," she said. "My sister loved apple pie."

I got her a slice so large it was unfit for human consumption, and we spent the next few hours at the table, refilling our glasses more than a few times as she told me about her sister. She didn't tell her stories in any particular order, but by the end, it felt like I really had known her, the anecdotes from every stage of their lives pouring out. And in them, I could feel her loss, the stories all ending with the same knowledge that there were no more memories to make.

My impression of Ellie's sister was that she had been a good time, a sort of chaotic good who never hesitated to have fun where she could find it. But I could see, too, how a rift could grow between two people without either of them meaning to, how it could be frustrating to be her sister even as it had led to all these stories. For example, down in Arkansas, when she was nine, her sister had started coaxing a bunch of raccoons closer and closer to their house with treats until there were a half-dozen of them in the kitchen one morning, tearing the place apart.

Finally, as the candle I'd set between us burned down to nothing, I realized I was drunk. I didn't make a habit of drinking anymore — mostly because the restaurant was barely breaking even as it was — but with a beautiful woman before me and the shop shimmering in the streetlights, I made a note to try it more often. Even if I'd have hell to pay for a hangover in the morning with the age of my poor liver…

"So," I asked, "what now? Can I walk you to the train?"

"Yeah," she said, draining what was left of her drink. "I ought to get back. I'm leaving for Arkansas in the morning."

"So soon?" I asked, trying to find the right mix of disappointment without sounding needy. Somehow, I'd thought she might stay, even if that was before her sister.

"My project's mostly done. I guess I was staying for my sister. And now…"

"Yeah," I said, nodding. "That makes sense."

She met my eyes, holding them for a long time. Then, she leaned in and kissed me. It was slow at first, our lips lingering together before it sped up, both of us standing at the same time, my hand finding the small of her back as she kissed me more deeply. I couldn't remember the last time I'd kissed someone, but we seemed to find our way just fine, our styles compatible enough as she led and I followed. Still, like the first bout of rain in a summer thunderstorm, it was over just as soon as it started. She pulled back, cupping a hand on my cheek.

"Sorry," she said, grinning. "I guess I needed that."

"Don't be," I said. "It was…an honor."

She straightened her blouse, running a hand through her hair.

"Maybe if things had been different, this could have been something."

"Yeah," I said, "maybe."

"I think I'll find my own way to the train. But if I ever come back, I know where I'll stop for pie."

"I'd like that," I said as she walked away. The doorbell chimed again, and just as quickly as she'd appeared, she was gone.

I slumped back into my chair, my mind blank as I sat in stunned silence, the whirring of the fridges in back the only sound. I wasn't sure how to feel — I'm still not, if I'm honest. Should I have done something different? I couldn't ask her to stay, not after one kiss with nothing keeping her here… Besides, relationship OCD loves a clean ending. Here, no one's heart had to get broken, no one had to cry — other than the tears she'd already shed.

But what would come after? In spite of everything, I felt…happy, like the last bubbles escaping from a leftover can. Did this mean I should try for love again? Or was my life enough as it was? I was here, in my city, in my restaurant. And in my own way, I *had* helped. I'd served pie to people who hadn't had it in ages, and I'd helped Ellie find her sister, even if she was gone. And in her time of need, even at my age and in my state of brokenness, at least I still had lips she could kiss.

I don't know if I've learned anything. I'm not even sure if there's anything *to* learn. But Ellie was right about one thing: The future of nothing is nothing. And as long as I'm here, so long as this silly thing called life keeps going on this spinning blue dot, my light will be on. If anyone needs me, or even if they just need pie, they know where I'll be.

THE END

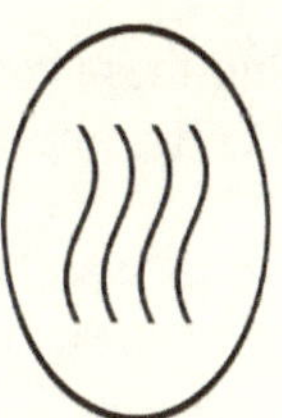

Thank you for joining me for *The Future is Nothing* and making it this far! I know this can all feel like a lot. It *is* a lot. But I don't want you to feel discouraged. I want you to get excited. Be a climate optimist.

If these stories inspired you to learn more about what you can do for the planet, please check out the web companion I mentioned in the dedication at https://jhtomen.com/the-future-of-nothing/ It has deep dives on the technology and philosophy behind these stories — and I hope it's something you'll find helpful!

We have a lot of challenges ahead, but everything humans have caused, we can also solve. We have the technology. We have the inspiration. All we need now is the will, the grit to say no to the way the world has always been and dream of the way it could be.

We need amazing people like you. People who read climate fiction and say, "Yes, that could be me." People who pick something from these stories to introduce into their life. I believe in you. I believe in us. Together, I know we can do this.

Thank you so much, for reading these stories, for caring about fiction, and for being you! You're amazing, and I'm so grateful the planet has you in it!

With love,
JH Tomen

www.ingramcontent.com/pod-product-compliance
Lightning Source LLC
Chambersburg PA
CBHW061551310726
48972CB00008B/2714